T0114295

Dear Readers,

I still remember the first time I read Donald Goines. The godfather of street lit, he was the first to write books about characters I could identify with. To some, the stories may have been aggressive, overly stylized, and even dangerous. But there was an honesty there—a realness. I made a vow that if I wrote a book or got into the publishing game, I would try the same one-two punch—that of a Daddy Cool or Black Gangster.

Last year my memoirs, *From Pieces to Weight,* marked the beginning. Now, I'm rounding up some of the top writers, same way I rounded up some of the top rappers in the game, to form **G-Unit** and take this series to the top of the literary world. The stories in the **G-Unit** series are the kinds of dramas me and my crew have been dealing with our whole lives: death, deceit, double-crosses, ultimate loyalty, and total betrayal. It's about our life on the streets, and no one knows it better than us. Not to mention, when it comes to delivering authentic gritty urban stories of the high and low life, our audience expects the best.

That's what we're going to deliver, starting with **Nikki Turner,** bestselling author of *Hustler's Wife* and *The Glamorous Life*; **Noire,** bestselling author of *G-Spot* and *Thug-A-Licious*; and finally **K. Elliott,** author of *Street Fame*.

You know I don't do anything halfway, and we're going to take this street lit thing to a whole other level. Are you ready?

BABY BROTHER

AN URBAN EROTIC APPETIZER

50 Cent and Noire

G Unit Books

NEW YORK   LONDON   TORONTO   SYDNEY

POCKET BOOKS, a division of Simon & Schuster, Inc.
1230 Avenue of the Americas, New York, NY 10020

ISBN-13: 978-1-4165-3202-6
ISBN-10:   1-4165-3202-1

First G-Unit/MTV/Pocket Books paperback edition January 2007

10 9 8 7 6 5 4 3 2 1

For information regarding special discounts for bulk purchases,
please contact Simon & Schuster Special Sales at 1-800-456-6798
or business@simonmandschuster.com

DEDICATION

To all the Baby Brothers who are out there navigating the urban jungles of Brooklyn, Queens, Manhattan, Staten Island, and the Bronx: Don't let the mean streets strangle you. Stay on the success grind and keep doin' the damn thang.

—Noire

ACKNOWLEDGMENTS

Father, thank you. Missy, Nisaa, Man, Jay, Tyrone, Angie, Aretha, and my girl Melissa Shaw from the Bronx, thanks for your loyalty and your love. 50 Cent, thanks for this opportunity and for your confidence in my skills. G-Unit Books is gonna kill 'em left and right! To Reem Raw and N.J.S. Entertainment, your gully beats and hot lyrics keep the ink flowing over my paper and the stories flowing from my soul. To my readers and fans, thanks for all the love and the calls and letters of support and concern. You shower it on me every day, and I'm giving it right back to you with each book I write. Check me out at www.myspace.com/asknoire and get ready to ride with me to the next level!

Stay Black,

Noire

BABY BROTHER

CHAPTER 1

Prisoner number 837R2006
Height, six feet, one inch
Face front.
(flash)
Turn to your left.
(flash)
Now to your right.
(flash)

"*Good morning, New York! It's time to get the hell outta bed! Right about now you're waking up with my girl Jonesy! Sure we hired her because she's pretty . . . but then after talking to her I realized she also has a great rap! Wake up on Hot 97! Let's get ta grinding on this hot, sunny morning in the Big Apple!*"

The early morning sun baked the run-down five-story tenement from the direction of Queens. On the second floor, thin red curtains swayed in the light breeze, and the B20 to Spring Creek groaned toward Linden Boulevard, traces of its exhaust fumes wafting through the open window.

Inside the bedroom, Baby Brother plunged into his wet yummy, bumping bone and scraping walls. "Yeahhhh," he groaned, getting his mash on. He took a deep breath, then grunted and arched his back, pounding his pipe.

Beneath him, Sari moaned and panted. Her dark hair curled around her face and fanned over the pillow. Her juices smelled like Fruity Pebbles and it was just about breakfast time.

"Right there, mami?" Veins bulging, Baby Brother demanded, flinging sweat. "Is that where you like it, baby? Right there?"

She tossed her head no, but still squealed in pleasure as he grabbed her toned thighs, spreading them apart in a wide V. His fingers were hot on her caramel-colored skin. She pulled him deeper into her, then whispered something nasty in Spanish as the headboard slammed against the wall and Miss Jonesy talked shit in the background.

"Cool," he said, withdrawing until only the head was left inside. It pulsed and throbbed in the rim of her tight opening as he extended his arms and balanced himself on the palms of his hands. "If the dick ain't good to ya then I might as well take it out."

She squeezed her legs tight. "No!"

He laughed. "Then let me hear you say this dick is good!"

"Shh!" She stopped rolling her ass and frowned. "Why you gotta say 'dick' so loud like that?! Tony might hear you!"

Baby Brother laughed again. "Fuck Tony."

Sari giggled and slapped his arm. Working her hips into a hard grind, she pulled him deeply into her soft gushy, then wrapped her long legs around his back as her teeth found his nipple. She swirled her wet tongue around his bud and sucked gently, her lips pressed firmly against the hard muscle of his chest.

Baby Brother clenched his jaw and shuddered. "Aaah, baby. Damn. Shit. Slow down. *Goddamn.* Slow down, mami! Damn you throwing some good-ass stuff around, girl."

It was sticky and hot inside her box and he didn't wanna move. He forced himself to pull out of her, then slid down her body, sighing. He paused to lick her stiff, light brown nipple, then continued south, lapping sweat from the crevice of her belly button before pressing his face deeply into her wet spot.

"Yummy . . ." He smacked between licks. Her juice was like honey. Sweet and thick, and he wished he could put his whole head up inside her.

Sari gasped. Her muscles went rigid as he made waves of pleasure flow from her center. She held tight to his head and opened her mouth. A Spanish pleasure tirade exploded from her lips and filled the whole room. "Aaah, baby! Yeah, just like that. Right there, just like that." Then moments later, "Oooweee, too deep! No, harder. Yeah. *Just like that!*" And then finally, "Oooh. Damn. Yeah. Damn! Why you gotta leave me, huh, Zabu? Why you gotta go? I love you, Z. You know that, don't you?"

Baby Brother moaned, spurting the last of himself into her warmth. He rolled onto his side and pulled her into his dark arms. He gazed into her flashing eyes, and despite the way their bodies had just battled, he saw the deep pain that was lurking there.

He kissed her damp curls and squeezed her closer. "I *gotta* go, girl. That's what's real. This ghetto's gonna kill me if I don't. But I'm coming back for you, Sari. That's truth, baby. That's truth."

━━   ━━   ━━   ━━

Baby Brother got up. He used a bunch of Wet Wipes to clean himself, then kissed Sari again and got dressed. It was time to go. Priest was waiting for him back at the crib and they had moves to make.

"I'ma get up with you later, cool? I'll be waiting downstairs around six. Have your fine ass ready too, 'cause the West Indian Day Parade draws niggahs from all over Brooklyn and there won't be noplace to park near Eastern Parkway."

He grinned at Sari, then walked over to the half-open window and raised it all the way up. He glanced down at the sparkling whip parked below, in the exact same condition he had left it in the night before. While Sari's eyes were on him he pretended like he was climbing out the window and onto the raggedy fire escape, but then turned around real fast and walked over to the door instead. He heard her shocked intake of breath as he reached for the knob.

"Z! What the hell you doing?" She jumped up, her eyes

flashing with alarm. He liked it when she got all hyped. Her nature was a perfect indicator of her ethnic mix. Black and Hispanic. She was a down chick and had a temper on her too. "Don't open that damn door! You gotta go out the window!" She snatched the sheet off the bed and tried to wrap it around her nakedness. "Man, Tony's home! You can't let him see you leaving outta my room!"

Baby Brother grinned and walked out, closing the door on her high-pitched protests. Fuck all that window action. He was leaving out the door today.

His light brown eyes danced and his skin looked chocolaty smooth against the red-and-white Rocawear shirt he wore. He hiked up his jeans until they settled over his Air Force Ones just the right way, then headed down the short hall toward the front door.

Passing the kitchen, he stuck his head inside then slammed his hand against the side of the refrigerator as hard as he could. A cracking sound exploded in the air, startling the handsome Puerto Rican killer sitting at the table. Out of nowhere, a small silver gat appeared in the man's hand.

"Damn, Tony! What? You gone shoot me or something?"

Tony stared at him with a snarl and set the gun

down on the chair between his thighs. Even in the heat his voice came out feeling like ice.

"Yo, muthafucka. What the fuck is you doin' in my crib?"

Baby Brother checked out Sari's half brother. Her father had been black, and while she was brown and curly-haired, Tony was a pale Hispanic with dark, piercing eyes. He'd been sitting alone in the kitchen smoking a dutchey and counting a large stack of chips. His jet-black hair was shower-wet, his bare chest stained with tattoos and bulging with jailhouse muscle. A large bag half-filled with white powder sat on the table in front of him, and another much smaller bag rested on a triple-beam scale.

"Damn. Whatever happened to 'good morning,' son?"

Tony pushed the stack of money aside and reached into his back pocket. The glint of his knife caught Baby Brother's eye.

"Yo. You been up in my joint all night?" His voice was deadly. "Back there witcha dick up in my little sister?" He twirled his knife. The tip of his blunt glared red, and his cold eyes never left Baby Brother's face. "You must be a bad motherfucker then, huh?"

Baby Brother laughed and held up his hands. "Chill, amigo. I ain't the enemy, son. Shit, after three years I'm just about family. Plus, I'm about to be outtie in a minute. No disrespect to your crib or nothing. I just wanted to spend some time with Sari. You know, treat her right before I leave, man."

Tony stopped twirling the knife. Baby Brother knew how sharp that blade was. Tony was almost as legendary as the Monster had been on the knife tip. Both of them had plenty of carved-up victims walking the streets of Brooklyn.

"That's right, I forgot. You graduated. Now you runnin' off to college to be some kinda fuckin' professor or something." He laughed coldly. "That's real stupid, yo. You need to claim you some territory and be a real man now, homey. You can fuck my little sister in my crib, then come stand in my kitchen where I can smell your nuts? Yeah, you a fuckin' man. But real men pay dues, amigo! Leave that college business for the herbs out in Canarsie and get yourself a grind. Business is good on this side of the bridge. Tell ya pretty-ass brothers you coming to work for me now."

"Fool, what I look like? You can kill all that shit. I got plans. I ain't slinging rock for nobody. Not for you, not for that stupid niggah Borne, and not for my brothers neither."

Tony laughed. "Okay, okay, I tell you what! I'm a nice mothafucker. Those fuckin' twins can come work for me too, cool? You can be my runner and your brothers can be my capos. You can hold my balls, while they take turns suckin' my dick!" He laughed louder this time, sweeping half the bills off the table and to the floor as he gripped his knife in his fist and glared.

Baby Brother watched him for a moment, then walked toward the door shaking his head. Tony had been tryna get at him for years, but it was cool. He was the oldest boy in the Santos's family, and Sari was the youngest and only girl. It was only right that he would look out for his little sister the same way the six older Davis brothers came to the table for him.

Baby Brother and Sari had been rolling together since he was in the tenth grade and she was in the ninth. They were on opposite sides of a family rivalry. The Davis twins, Farad and Finesse, controlled the rock and the powder flowing in and out of Brownsville and were well-known for their savage brutality. The Santos clan ran the streets of East New York, with Tony at the helm. He was ruthless and crazy. A cutter. Like the Monster. A loose missile just itching to launch. There was no love lost between the two families, but they tolerated each other. Mainly on account of business, and partly because of Baby Brother and Sari.

Baby Brother walked down the hall and went through the stairwell door. The hot smell of stale urine and beer rushed out at him. He maneuvered around a couple of winos and crackheads who were sitting on the stairs trying to come down off their all-night highs.

"Whassup, Felix. Big Porter. How you doin' this morning, Mrs. Woodson?"

The woman he addressed beamed at him. She was Jelly's moms, a dude he knew from way back in the day. They'd boxed together at the BBC gym, but Jelly had gone into the Marine Corps two years ago, and it wasn't long after that that the streets had claimed his mother.

"Baby Brother!" the woman exclaimed. She pulled her bra strap up on her shoulder and tried to smooth her hair. "You almost ready to leave us, huh?" She nudged the crackhead sitting next to her. "This boy right here is something else. He used to be Jelly's best friend, you know. He was the only kid who ever whupped my Jelly in the ring too. Now he's going off to college to learn how to be an astronaut! Ain't that right, Baby Brother?"

He smiled down at her. Her hair was raggedy and

her teeth looked like rotten little worms, but Baby Brother showed her much respect.

"Nah, Mrs. Woodson. I'm gonna be a surgeon. I'm majoring in premed." The odors assaulting him were excruciatingly foul, but he withstood them. He stood there and carried on a conversation with Mrs. Woodson the same way he used to when his boy Jelly had still been around. He talked to her the way he used to talk to her back when she was still a loudmouthed, heavyset, dark-skinned woman holding her family down in a cool apartment off of New Lots Avenue and pushing a decent whip. As cracked-out as Mrs. Woodson was now, and as dreadful as she smelled, Baby Brother treated her the same way he would've wanted somebody to treat his own mother if he'd had one.

"Boy, you got a future ahead of you," Jelly's moms told him. "A real future. Wherever you goin' to school, hurr' up and get there. This place ain't for boys like you. Don't let it crush you like it done crushed me."

―― ―― ―― ――

Baby Brother stepped out of the building and into the hazy sunshine. He inhaled the morning air and gazed at the candy-red 2007 drop-top Mercedes parked at the curb. The whip was just like he'd left it and he wasn't surprised. Everybody in Central Brooklyn knew Farad's wheels when they saw them, and only a fool with a death wish would have laid a finger on the paint.

"Baby Brother!"

His name rang out from a doorway across the street.

"You tell that niggah Farad his g-ride ain't as tight as mine!"

Baby Brother grinned and lifted his chin at the skinny brother standing on the stoop. It was Bip, one of Farad's ex-partners. A guy who had grown up with the Davis brothers in Brownsville, but who slummed around in East New York now. Bip had been banned from Brownsville on the direct word of Farad. He'd been allowed to keep his life because they'd been dawgs damn near from the cradle. But even that wouldn't stop Farad from having him murked if he got caught crossing over into The Ville.

"That's truth, Bip. I'ma let him know that shit too."

"Yeah. Let him know I been up watching his whip all night, yo. Tell him he owe me! If it wasn't for me some base-head prolly woulda ran off with his spinners."

Baby Brother unlocked the car and climbed behind the wheel. It was a quality ride, paid for with cash dollars. Farad had it detailed every three days, and it smelled factory-fresh at all times. He settled into the seat, then slid the key in the ignition and listened to the engine purr.

He drove down the streets of East New York with the top down, driving aimlessly and absorbing the hood vibe. N.J.S. beats blared from the speakers as Reem Raw killed a hot track with illa East Coast lyrics. He rode up Shepherd, crossed Linden Boulevard, and headed toward New Lots. It was early, but niggahs was already out on the hot streets scheming on their next hustle.

Baby Brother nodded at a few familiar faces as he cruised down the block. He stopped at a light on the corner of Hegeman Avenue. A couple of gangsta-looking niggahs with larceny in their eyes grilled him as they walked by. Baby Brother was up on them. He knew what they were thinking and hoped they were smart enough to think again. He was a hard niggah, and good with his hands. He'd come up on the streets and in the gym, trained by his brothers to get in close and handle his.

But with two days left in New York he wasn't trying to get into nothing hot except some more of

Sari's yummy. He pumped the volume even higher and decided to let Farad's whip speak loud and clear to anybody who might wanna get smoked.

On the way home he thought a lot about college and about Sari too. Leaving her was gonna be hard, but he knew it would pay off in the end. A degree from Stanford came with certain guarantees, and although he was gonna miss his brothers around, he was grateful for the opportunity to escape the urban jungle. It's what their mother would have wanted. Their father too.

Pulling over at a corner candy store beneath the Number 3 El, Baby Brother went inside and bought a soda and a bag of pretzels. When he came back out a bunch of kids were admiring Farad's whip. He let them climb inside and blow the horn and push a few buttons and shit, then he got behind the wheel again and made his way back to The Ville, where his brothers waited.

CHAPTER 2

Priest had just finished his breakfast of buttery grits and eggs when the front door slammed. Three of Farad's soldiers were posted outside, and relief flooded Priest as he heard familiar footsteps approaching. Baby Brother had stayed in East New York all night long, and even though the kid was eighteen now, Priest still worried about him, especially out there messing around with them treacherous Puerto Ricans.

"Zabu!" he called out, his voice heavy and full of bass. "You late, man. I told you I was gone take you to get some suitcases today, but if you wanna haul your gear to Cali in some black garbage bags, you can do that, you know."

Despite his bark Priest's eyes were full of pride as his youngest brother strolled into the kitchen. Just like his six brothers, Baby Brother was tall, with deep mahogany skin and amber eyes. He was muscled up and perfectly cut, and although they all worked out hard, the majestic physique was just part of their genetics.

Priest was the oldest and the most battle-scarred.

He had raised the other boys after their mother died, and Baby Brother was his heart. His favorite. His salvation. Priest couldn't help it. These days he served as an assistant pastor of a small storefront church, operated his own barbershop up on Rockaway Avenue, and gave Bible lessons at a youth center twice a week.

But he had a past that just couldn't be wiped clean. He had pimped women, slung rock, slumped foes, organized gangs, and hustled the hell outta the game. But looking at Baby Brother killed all those past demons. His little brother was his pride and joy. Hard evidence that despite all the grimy capers Priest had pulled, all the prey he'd bitten, and all the upstate prison time he'd served, that somehow God had favored him and allowed him to redeem himself and do something right. Every time he looked at Baby Brother Priest saw the man that he himself should have been.

"What it do, 'Twan." Baby Brother gave him some dap on his way to the refrigerator.

"You late, man. I told you we was leaving at nine."

Baby Brother flashed him a grin and rubbed his stomach. "I'm hungry, tho'. Gotta stick something in my belly before we roll."

Priest opened the microwave and took out one of

four paper plates he'd covered in Saran Wrap. "Here." He set it on the table. "Put ya face in this and hurry up. I gotta be back for services this afternoon."

"Aiight. Yo, why's it so quiet in here? Where is everybody?"

Priest shrugged. "You know the scene, man. When you do your work under the dark of night you gotta regroup when it's light. The twins are both upstairs. Matter fact, Malik's gone be here in a minute. Go upstairs and tell them two knuckleheads to get down here and eat."

Ten minutes later Priest sat at the head of the table watching four of his young brothers grub. Malik had arrived dressed in his NYPD blues, and as they dug into the plates he'd prepared for them Priest couldn't help but smile inside. It felt good to sit at the same table with his cats. Raheem had taken a trip for the long weekend, and Kadir was down in A.C. doing his thing, but with Baby Brother leaving for college in a couple of days, both of them would be showing up to see him off.

"Snatch 'em!" Malik hollered real loud.

"Guard ya plate!" Baby Brother threw his arms on the table, encircling his breakfast with wary eyes.

"Man, keep your hands off my damn food!" Farad

complained, setting his fork down. "I ain't playin that 'snatch 'em' shit today, dawg. You betta chill with that."

Malik laughed and stuck the stolen slice of turkey bacon in his mouth. "You ain't gotta play nothing but defense, man. You know the rules, muhfuckah! Lose ya heat, I snatch ya meat!"

Laughter rang out around the table and Farad reacted quickly.

"Snatch 'em!"

Finesse cursed as his twin snatched a crisp slice of bacon off his plate and started crunching.

"You getting slow, niggah," Farad chuckled. "I coulda got me two pieces off you, yo."

Priest laughed along with them, but his heart was heavy. He had prayed for a better life for his brothers. Nothing would make him happier than seeing Farad and Finesse out of the game and doing something legitimate with their skills. He'd dreamed of opening a chain of barbershops and installing one of his brothers at the helm of each operation, but Raheem and Malik both had good jobs with benefits, Kadir was hooked on card tables, and neither of the twins was interested in a nine-to-five. Priest stood up and refilled Baby Brother's glass from a container of juice on the counter.

"So," he said, looking around the table before nodding at his youngest brother. "Everybody 'bout ready to get rid of this lil son? Ain't but two days left, then he's out."

Finesse shrugged. "I'd rather see him bounce for a minute than have him scrambling yay like them niggahs on the stoop. Damn, B-Brother. You gone be on some real West Coast shit when you get back. You sure you can't go to school somewhere in New York? Maybe upstate?"

"I can go almost anywhere I wanna go," Baby Brother said. "But Stanford is giving up the best scholarship package, man. Plus it's a top school. I'd be crazy to let something like this slide by me."

Malik nodded, wiping his mouth. "That's what's real, man. Graduate from Stanford with a degree in shit shoveling and you still considered a heavyweight in the corporate world. Fuck around with one of these city schools and you might end up working for Transit or coming on the force, or worse—following Ra down to Corrections and getting on over there." He tossed his plate in the trash. "Cali is a good bet for you. Go for it. We got your back."

"Yeah," Farad said, standing up with his empty plate

in his hand. He reached over and punched Baby Brother on his shoulder, then mushed his head like he was ten years old again. "Just make sure you put some damn gas in my car before you fly, though. Shit! I'm glad that niggah leaving. I'ma finally get a chance to push my own whip."

Malik headed for the door. "Yo, Ant, what time we flying outta here on Monday?"

"Seven. I already told Ra to be here by four. That'll put us at JFK way before five."

"Cool." Malik nodded. "I'll get wit'chall in a few. They got me pulling a double shift so it's gone be a long night."

Fifteen minutes later two of the Davis brothers were ready to hit downtown Brooklyn. Priest let Baby Brother drive. He couldn't bring himself to get behind the wheel of Farad's drug-bought car. Negativity was all up in it, and he wanted no part of that.

As they pulled out of the driveway, Priest looked back at the four-bedroom home his mother had scraped to buy for them after their father's murder. It shamed him to remember all the hoes and drugs and hot gats he'd brought in and out of these rooms back in the day when he was living like a dog and didn't give a damn.

His brothers Raheem and Malik shared a crib in Crown Heights, and Kadir was living down in A.C. These days it was the twins, Farad and Finesse, who were shaming their mother's house, running a drug empire from her very bedroom, but there wasn't much Priest could do or say about it. Hell, he'd set them up in the game. Taught them how to hustle on the success tip, and helped them earn their deadly reps.

But when Priest got knocked and sent upstate, things changed. He was locked down for almost two years before the Lord touched his soul and changed his heart. The prison chaplain had mentored him and helped him adjust his outlook on life, and by the time he was released that monstrous killer inside him was dead and Priest had been born. Ministry lived in his heart where menace and mischief had once run amok.

He sat back in his seat and glanced at Baby Brother. California was a long way away and he was gonna miss him, but it was a life or death thing that he go. Zabu was untouched by the poisons of their world. Unaffected by the lure of the streets that seemed to strangle Brooklyn boys like him by the tens of thousands.

Priest ran his hand down his sweaty face and let out a deep breath. *He's almost there, Mama,* he thought.

Like his other brothers, Priest had made a promise to his mother on her deathbed. They'd stood over her wasted body and held hands and vowed that no matter what happened to them, they'd stay together and make something good come outta their lives. They had told their mother not to worry. Said everything she needed to hear, easing her heart so she could die in peace. And at the very end they had promised to do the last and most important thing that she had asked.

They promised to take care of Baby Brother.

— — — —

Later that night Eastern Parkway was packed. Everybody in Brooklyn knew that the biggest and hottest event on Labor Day weekend was the West Indian Day Parade. Cameron Davis, Baby Brother's father, had been from Jamaica. He had come to New York as a teenager, and even though he'd been killed when Baby Brother was just a tyke, his brothers had painted a colorful picture of their father and made sure that shit was cemented in Baby Brother's mind.

Cameron was a true hood legend. Even to this day, just the mention of his name could strike awe in an

OG's eyes. He'd been a slick gambler with a fearsome rep. They had lived in the projects, but Cameron kept his family in the finest condition and they didn't want for a damn thing. Reva Davis was known for the African diamonds her husband draped her in. Her mink coats were legendary, and some said she had a different one for each day of the week. Others went even further than that. They said Cameron had stacked so much paper down in A.C. that the feds were hounding him for tax evasion because he was technically unemployed, but kept at least three late-model cars on the curb at all times.

Out of all the tales Baby Brother had heard about his father, one fact stayed consistent. He had loved his sons. He called his boys his lucky seven, and he would have died for them and their mother if need be.

But as hard as Cameron was, he still wasn't bulletproof. He'd gotten popped behind a jealous niggah and a shady bet, and life for the Davis crew had taken a downhill turn from there.

Eastern Parkway was live when Baby Brother and Sari rolled up. After circling around side streets for almost an hour, Baby Brother found a parking spot on the far side of Lincoln Terrace Park. It was hot and sticky and festive as hell. The steel bands were pounding out that melodic island rhythm, and calypso music played loudly in the air, and dancers and revelers spilled down the middle of the street. There were endless floats and sound trucks inching down the middle of the large urban parkway, and crowds of people lined up along the service road, drinking brew, smoking sticky, and getting wild.

They stopped at a food stand and Baby Brother got Sari a taste of jerk chicken, a piece of coconut bread, and some mauby to drink. He pointed out flags from Trinidad, Jamaica, Barbados, and Grenada. They came up close near a band wildin' out on steel drums and started dancing with the crowd. Baby Brother grabbed Sari's shoulders and turned her around. She had on a bright pink clingy halter top that showed the imprint of her nipples, and a pair of pale pink shorts that set off her brown skin just right.

"Come on, girl." He laughed, trying to make her smile. She was still on that "why-you-gotta-go" shit and he wanted her to chill and have a good time. "Wind that shit up!" he told her, eyeing her firm hips. "Do that thing you be doing when you stand over me on the bed."

Sari laughed and turned around so he could see her

round ass. She started winding her thick wicked like an island girl, working that heavy West Indian beat like she had a few drops of Jamaica in her blood.

"Yeah, that's it, mami," Baby Brother said, biting his lower lip as he watched her move. He stepped up behind her, letting that bouncy ass rub against his hardening dick. He never got tired of looking at her or digging in her either. She was brown and dimpled and sexy as hell. Phatty ass, bomb titties, tiny waistline with a tight stomach and a deep navel. He loved the hell outta her, and already he was thinking about getting back to New York for Christmas. He was gonna be doing plenty of pillow-fucking until then, though, 'cause he wasn't planning to slum around on his honey.

"Sell that shit!" somebody yelled nearby. "Hold up— I think I already bought some a' that stuff last night!"

Baby Brother took his eyes off Sari's ass and grilled the cat that had spoken. He recognized him immediately. Borne Reynolds. Baby Brother kept his hands on Sari's shoulders, but his lips had turned down in a hard frown.

"Yo, who the fuck you talkin' to?" he barked, his voice heavy with bass. Unlike Farad and Finesse— dealers who lived and breathed their hustle from the trenches—Borne was one of them bitch rollers. A high-bank slanger who kept his hands clean and let his crew do all his dirty work. He was becoming a real headache on the streets and Baby Brother had heard his brothers discussing how to handle him. Borne ran a rival drug click on the border of East New York and Brownsville called the Brooklyn Bornes, and not only was Sari's brother Tony and his click gunning for him, the Davis brothers were getting tired of him and his crew too.

Borne laughed as Baby Brother stared him down. "Oh, my bad. Sorry, my man. I didn't see who you was for a minute. I ain't tryna disrespect your little taco or nothing, homey, so don't go running telling them bitch-ass brothers of yours nothing tryna start no war."

"Man, fuck you," Baby Brother said as Sari backed up into him, pushing against him as she walked backward, putting distance between him and Borne. Baby Brother never even associated with the happenings between Borne and his brothers, but he knew these streets were mean and it didn't matter. He had to either stand firm for his, or be disrespected by fools like this. "Just watch what the fuck comes outta ya mouth when my lady is present, dig?"

Borne laughed again, backing away and into the

crowd. "I'm feeling you, chief. You got that good Puerto Rican yummy on lock and don't want nobody else to get none. I swear to God she look like this bitch I had on a leash this morning, though. Look just like her around the muzzle, yo!"

Pushing Sari aside, Baby Brother lunged into the crowd.

"No!" Sari screamed, clutching his shirt and pulling him back. She wrapped her arms around him from behind and lowered her weight, digging her feet in. Baby Brother stared at the spot where Borne had just mocked him. The crowd had swallowed Borne's laughing face, but had not erased the sound of his voice from Baby Brother's ears.

"That motherfucker need to chill. . . ." he growled, his chest heaving. "If I see his ass out here again, it's going down."

Sari continued to hold him from behind, and when he turned around and put his arms around her in return, she looked up into his face and spoke. "You didn't come this far in life by charging after every sucker who pops shit, Z. You know how it goes down out here. We're targets, baby. My brother's got crazy enemies in this game, both your brothers got crazy enemies in this game. There's always gonna be somebody trying to press them by fuckin' with us. Just let it go, Zabu. We came out to have a good time, right?"

He nodded, then grinned.

"Good," Sari said, smiling in return. "So fuck Borne. He wasn't in them sheets while you did your thing this morning, now was he?"

"Nah." Baby Brother laughed and slapped Sari on the ass. "And he ain't gonna be in them with us tonight neither."

With the drama over, they moved onward through the crowd toward Franklin Avenue, enjoying the sights, sounds, and smells while Crown Heights got its party on. Baby Brother was in the lead as they wormed inch by inch through the thick, boisterous revelers. He was pulling Sari along with her hand grasped firmly in his when he felt a jerk and his hand was empty.

"Sari!" He turned around and saw her craning her neck, looking through the crowd. She was holding her shirt up to her neck, and the strings of her halter were dangling by her arms.

"Motherfuckers!" she spat. "Somebody untied my strings!"

"Did you see who did it?"

She shook her head no.

Baby Brother scanned the crowd wildly. There were so many people doing so many different things that it was impossible to pinpoint the culprit, but after having those words with Borne he was about ready to wild out and start swinging on any damn body.

"C'mere," he said, turning her around and taking her pink halter strings in his hands. She lifted her hair and he tied a double knot behind her neck, making sure it couldn't be pulled free with just a tug.

"Walk in front of me," he said, guiding her through the crowd ahead of him. They made it down past Nostrand Avenue without any further problems, and by the time they got to Franklin Avenue they were in a good mood again and enjoying the atmosphere.

They partied on Eastern Parkway until late night, then drove over to a club in Bed-Stuy. Sari had switched up from the Coronas she'd bought from a bodega near the parade, and was now drinking Patrón. Baby Brother wasn't about to take a chance on fucking up Farad's whip. He let his woman get her head buzzed while he drank Pepsi and stayed straight.

"I'ma get my dance on right now!" Sari said, rocking her hips like a brown-skinned Shakira. Niggahs in the club was clocking her, but they did that shit from a distance because Baby Brother was all up on it, making his status known. "'Cause I ain't coming to the club no more until you get back home for Christmas."

He laughed as she killed her pink shorts, making his pants brick up. "The way you like to shake that ass girl? Nah, baby. Don't stay home waitin' around on me. You like to dance, mami. Don't matter if I'm gone. Come on out and dance."

Sari stopped dancing and stood still in the middle of the crowd. Her eyes flashed.

"Now why you say some shit like that, Z?" she screamed on him, waving her hand in his face. "What's really going on, huh? What the fuck you tryna tell me? You sending me out to the club because that's where you gonna be yourself?"

"Man . . ." Baby Brother looked around, exasperated. Sari was tipsy and off the fuckin' hook. Yeah, she could get jealous and hotheaded when she got buzzed, but he couldn't believe his girl was playin' herself like this. People dancing next to them were starting to stare, and a couple of niggahs in the crowd gave him the clown look.

"Baby why you trippin' like this? You knew this day

was coming! We planned for this shit! Studied together! Swore we would both make it up outta here! Next year you gonna be leaving for college too. Come out West when you graduate, baby. We can be together, girl. We *gonna* be together, Sari, damn!"

Sari was acting extra insecure and Baby Brother couldn't understand that shit. He was a stand-up nig- gah. He loved her, and had already proven that shit with his actions. Besides, as fine as Sari was, there wasn't no need for her to worry about him pushing up in no other freak's gushy. He was pussy-bitten to the max. Doped up on Sari. Strung out on everything about her. They'd been tight for three years, and he saw forever in their future. But he saw the glazed look in Sari's teary eyes. She wasn't really a drinker, and chugging back that Patrón on top of all them Coronas musta had her head going hard.

"Chill," he comforted her, hugging her close to his chest and letting her cling to him. "You hungry, baby? Let's go get something to eat."

Baby Brother drove toward a little chicken joint off Utica Avenue, but there was a crowd outside when they got there.

"Just take me home," Sari said before he could park the car.

"What's up? Oh, it's too crowded? Nah, all them nig-gahs ain't in line, baby. They just standing around tryna pick up some birds. It ain't gonna take that long." He opened his door and swung his long legs out, then stood up and leaned back in. "C'mon. Get out. I'm hungry."

Sari crossed her arms and sat right there. "I said I wanna go home, Z. I don't want no damn chicken. I just wanna go home."

Baby Brother couldn't call it. Sari could be real evil when she was drinking, but right now she was fuckin' with his head.

"Look. You need to come down off that crazy shit. I ain't going home hungry, so if you wanna sit up in here and wait, cool."

He slammed the car door and strode angrily toward the crowd, trying to determine which of these niggahs was on line, and who was just fuckin' loitering. He was moving through the bodies when he heard the noise.

"What the fuck?" he said, whirling around.

Sari was sitting in the driver's seat, leaning on the horn. Blinged-out birds in the crowd stuck their fingers in their ears, then started cuttin' up, talking shit.

"Get the fuck off that horn, bitch! Quit making all that fuckin' noise!"

Baby Brother strode back over to the whip and snatched the door open. "Yo what the fuck is you doing, Sari?"

She kept on beeping.

"Sari! Sari! SARI!"

She came up off the horn and looked at him. "I told you to take me home, Z. Now take me the fuck home."

Baby Brother waited until she slid over, then got back in the ride, ignoring the niggahs who was standing outside laughing at him. Maybe it was a good thing he was about to put some space between himself and Sari, he thought for a hot second. But then he squashed that shit. He knew Sari. The only reason his girl was wildin' was because she loved him and hated to see him leave.

He drove down the mostly empty streets with his mind heavy. Every now and then he glanced over at Sari, but her face was set and she refused to even look at him. Fuck! It was already early Sunday morning, and in a little more than twenty-four hours he would be on a plane flying out West. He didn't wanna leave Sari behind with shit hanging between them. What he really wanted to do was go back to her spot and dig up in her belly again. Maybe get him a little top, go down and rummage in her bottom. He'd even climb out the window and jump from the fire escape, if that's the way she wanted it.

Fuck it.

He looked ahead. They drove into East New York from Blake Avenue and turned down Pennsylvania until they hit New Lots. He turned right on Van Siclen, then pulled off the street and parked in an empty space behind a white truck.

"Look, Sari. You ain't really mad at me, girl. I know what's really going on, baby. You just feelin' some hurt behind me leaving, right?"

Sari surprised him, whirling in her seat to face him.

"Oh, you think it's about you 'cause you going to college, right, Z? What the fuck am I, some strung-out little charity case? My life ain't gone stop just because you bounce outta Brooklyn, Zabu. Don't fuckin' hype yourself like that. Just take me home."

Baby Brother scratched his damn head. Here he was trying to be sensitive to her feelings and she flips the whole cake on him.

"I don't know why you trippin', Sari, but you need to trust me—"

"Kiss my ass!" Sari shrieked, tears in her eyes. "Take

me home, Z. No, wait. Fuck you!" She flung the car door open and stomped out, leaving her Coach purse on the seat. "I don't need your ass. I know my way."

She started walking up the street, heading toward Schenk Avenue. Baby Brother drove alongside her, pouring his heart out.

"Get in the car, Sari. Come on, girl. I'll take you home."

She igged him.

"Sari, come on. For real. Quit this shit. I'm feeling you deep. You my heart." Sari crossed the street and Baby Brother did a ride-through at the stop sign. He leaned across the seat and kept on begging from the window.

"I'ma miss you real bad too, ya know. This shit ain't easy for me. You been everything to me, Sari. Girl I thought you knew that."

She was melting. He could tell by the way she walked. He kept the conversation going. Telling her how planted she was in his heart. How much he felt for her. Telling her the truth.

There was no more stride on her now. She was walking kinda slow, dragging her feet a little bit.

"Come on, mami. Get back in the car. I'll take you

home, if that's where you wanna go. I'll do whatever you want, Sari. You mean just that much to me, girl."

Baby Brother held his breath as she stopped, then turned to face him.

"This is not the end for us, is it, Z? I mean, you told me before that it was you and me forever."

"And I meant it too. This ain't the end, Sari. It's only the beginning. That's hard body truth, girl. Believe."

He sighed as she stepped toward the car. With his foot holding the brake, Baby Brother reached over and opened the door for her, and just as she reached out to grab it, a shot rang out in the still morning air, destroying the calm that had just come down over Sari and shattering Baby Brother's heart.

"Sari!" She collapsed straight to the ground in a heap. He jumped from the whip, ignoring it as it continued to roll forward until it collided into the back of a parked truck.

Baby Brother rushed to her side. She'd landed facedown, and he cried out when he turned her over and saw the blood slowly staining her shirt. Something clinged just a few yards away. Metal on metal. And then footsteps. Running.

He looked up and glimpsed a figure running up the

block. Rage gripped him. He jumped to his feet, leaving Sari where she lay. Less than fifty yards away he saw it. Barely breaking stride, Baby Brother reached down and scooped up the pistol the shooter had tried to toss into a storm drain. He ran hard. Catching up. He was a young black man in the ghetto who had never fired a weapon in his life. Now he fired three times. Quick. Bak! Bak! Bak!

He missed three times.

The shooter turned the corner and Baby Brother lost him.

Five seconds later he rounded the corner himself, heart pounding. Searching. *He's hiding in a fuckin' doorway!* Baby Brother's street senses screamed. He headed deeper into the darkness, his eyes sweeping doorways as he passed. But halfway down the block, tires squealed and suddenly the street lit up behind him.

"Drop your weapon! Drop your weapon and put your hands in the air!"

Baby Brother stood frozen. Numb.

"Sari," he whispered as an image of her bloody body flashed across his mind. His baby was down. Bleeding. He had to go help her.

He turned around and immediately squinted and

tried to shield his eyes with his hand. There were three squad cars. Headlights on high. Blinding him.

"I said drop the fuckin' weapon!"

Baby Brother knew they had the burners out. Trained on him and ready to body him at the slightest provocation. Suddenly the big picture clicked into focus. He was fucked. Not only was the shooter about to get away, there was a bloody body laying next to his car, just a block away. Baby Brother shuddered, then steeled himself for the worst. Sari was down, and his heart couldn't conceive of it. Everything he'd ever worked for had just crumbled to pieces in the blink of an eye. Shit was crazy. It couldn't be happening. The woman he loved had just gotten popped. But what was worse was the fact that Baby Brother was standing there covered in her blood. And holding the murder weapon.

CHAPTER 3

It was almost time for a shift change and even though Malik Davis was pulling a double, he felt ready to bring it down for the night. He walked a pretty decent beat and was cool with most of the criminals who lived in his sector. He'd been raised on these urban streets and he knew them well. Most of the knuckleheads he busted had either grown up with him or gone to school with him. It coulda got kinda tight busting brothahs he used to run with, but he tried hard to maintain a good relationship with everybody, and even when he had to cuff a niggah it was done with such affable respect that it was all good.

He was looking forward to taking off for the next few days. Baby Brother was going off to college on Monday, and him and his brothers Antwan and Raheem were gonna fly out West with him and make sure everything was straight.

Malik was proud of his youngest brother. Already he was achieving more than the rest of them had put together. Yeah, he had a decent grind as a NYPD cop, and most of the other Davis boys was holding it down pretty righteous, not counting the twins, but Baby Brother was special and he bragged about that kid to anybody who would listen.

He was pushing through the precinct doors as his man Wiley was coming out. "Yo. Whattup, Wile. You working a double tonight?"

Wiley reached out and put his hand on Malik's shoulder, urging him to turn around and walk back out the door. "I need to holla at you real quick before you go in there, bruh. I got some bad news."

Malik stared at Wiley, apprehension rising in his gut at the look on his man's face.

"What's poppin'?"

"It's your brother, man."

Malik sighed. Farad? Nah, probably Finesse. Two-strike felon, and busted again.

"Yo, he smoked a girl," Wiley went on, shaking his head. "Gunned her down in the street. They caught him holding the burner, man, with blood all over him."

Damn, was all Malik could think as his heart sank. Their moms was probably turning over in her grave. But something just didn't feel right about this. Finesse was brutal, but he had never been violent toward women.

He couldn't think of one reason his brother would have to pop no female. It just didn't add up. He shook his head. It was hard being a street cop and having two major drug dealers for brothers. They was extra tight, and he would lay down and die for either one of them, but sometimes living with the bullshit in their lives was real hard.

"They got him down at Central Booking," Wiley said. "I just figured you'd wanna know."

Twenty minutes later Malik had rolled up at Central Booking and was skimming a roster looking for his brother's name. He had a few boys who were on shift, but none of them remembered seeing one of his brothers being brought in. Malik got with a cop he knew from Van Dyke projects who gave him their prisoner log. He was dragging his finger down the paper and checking the long, detailed list for recent arrests when his eyes slid over a familiar name. What he saw made his hands shake and his mouth go dry. Prisoner number 837R2006 was not Finesse. It wasn't Farad either. It was Davis, Zabu Xade.

Finesse studied the young girl who was bobbing her head in his lap. She claimed he was her first, but he couldn't tell it. She gave top like a professional. He watched his joint sliding past her lips and disappearing into her mouth and wondered how the fuck she took it all without choking.

He pushed the flat of his palm against her forehead, raising her up. This bitch was a liar. Wasn't no cherry in her throat. She had this neck game on lock. Her technique was too tight to be light.

He had to chastise her. Storyteller. Scratch a liar and find a hoe. He slid both hands through her hair, his fingertips colliding with glued-in tracks. Winding up two fistfuls, he gripped her weave and stood, pulling her up with him.

"Get outta them clothes, girl."

The young girl giggled, then turned her back on him and shot him a smoky look over her shoulder. She was wearing a canary-colored belly-shirt and a matching skirt in a slinky, flowing material. She slid the shirt upward, the toned muscles in her stomach clenching and unfurling. Her firm young breasts practically jumped free when she pulled the shirt over her head, and Finesse sucked his bottom lip, loving her moves. She inched the bright yellow skirt down over her hips, tantalizing him with enticing gyrations. She was naked underneath and Finesse swore there was a trail of steam seeping from the triangle between her legs.

He'd seen enough. He turned her around and bent her over. "Let me in baby," he barked, pushing himself into her as deeply as he could. Yeah, she was a liar 'cause he'd slid right in. They went at it stroke for stroke. Her hands were on her breasts as she squeezed and flicked her own nipples. Finesse panted and pounded. He felt his nut rising. It turned him on to see her so turned on. He was about to lose it. His eyes was fluttering, his toes was curling, and he was just about ready to erupt when his cell phone rang.

"Shit!" He pumped real hard, almost there.

The cell jangled again, but this time shit sank in. This wasn't no regular call. His phone was spittin' a special tone. One reserved for the most crucial, dire emergencies. A tone that demanded his immediate attention. A matter of life or death.

He slapped the girl on the ass, snatching his pipe out of her and putting a freeze on both of their nuts. He grabbed the phone off a table and flipped it open.

"Who?" he demanded, and the response on the

other end of the line not only wilted his erection, it damn near stopped his heart.

"What?!?" With the phone still pressed to his ear, he pushed his soft dick back down inside his boxers. He shook his head, trying to clear it. He couldn't even wrap his mind around the shit Malik was telling him on the line, and a steely mask came down over his face as rage settled in his nuts. They'd gotten the wrong one. The *wrong* one. Somebody was about to get fuckin' blasted and Finesse was ready to spark shit off.

"Initiate the chain, muthafuckah," he told his brother. "I'm rolling out."

— — — —

Farad blacked the fuck out.

He was in Riverdale Houses playing Spades with some homeys when the Chirp came through. The score pad said Us and Them, and of course Farad was on the winning team. Game was five hundred, and they had 430 on the board and had taken a blind seven. His partner had just cut a book and saved them from getting set, and now he had come back in diamonds and was waiting for Farad's next play.

But the Nextel was pressed to Farad's ear and he couldn't see shit and he couldn't hear shit neither. The only thing that got through to him was the voice on the other end of the line.

"You sure, man?" he finally managed to say. "Malik you gotta be wrong, niggah. C'mon. Tell me you got your information wrong."

"I just seen him, man," Malik said, sounding close to tears. "They got him in a fuckin' holding cell, man. A pissy little holdin' cell with all kinda foul motherfuckers up in there with him."

Farad cursed. "Don't even worry about them niggahs, Leek. Baby Brother can hold shit down with his hands, man. That's truth, niggah. He'll be all right for a good minute, but what we gotta worry about now is getting him the fuck outta there."

He heard Malik take a deep breath. "Aiight. Let me see what I can do. He's gone be having an initial hearing in a little bit. I'll get down there early and talk to the judge. See if I can work something out for bail or whatever. But I don't know man . . . they charging him with murder, yo—"

"Just try," Farad interrupted forcefully, knowing how slim the odds were that a judge would agree to something like that. But for real tho, with Sari dead and her psycho brother motherfucker Tony on the loose, it mighta been better to just leave Baby Brother where he was for a minute. Fuck no! "Yeah, Leek. Just get your ass in there and try."

— — — —

Ain't this some shit! Kadir thought, laughing out loud. This big-ass fuckin' white boy was pissin' down his leg. Scared like that. The little one was scared too, but at least he wasn't pissin'. He was standing against the warehouse wall with a resigned look on his face like, "Shoot me if you wanna, niggah, but I'ma go out holding my nuts."

"Y'all eating lead tonight, motherfuckers," Kadir taunted. Motherfuckers just didn't learn. Gambling was a fuckin' disease, and nobody knew that better than him. Some people inherited heart disease, and others inherited cancer. Kadir was his father's son. He had inherited the betting disease, and just like Cameron, he had a sixth sense about the odds and was a top shark in the game of chance.

But no matter how much his hunches paid off, there was always some low-level motherfuckers who got in over their heads. Idiots like these two here, who took one look at him and pegged him as a pretty niggah who could be dicked around like an herb.

They weren't the first two to make that mistake, and they probably wouldn't be the last. There was something about the thrill of the bet that made niggahs get stupid. White boys too. Overstating a bet and floundering at the table was no crime. It could happen to anybody. But trying to stiff a cat like him outta his cash was an unforgivable atrocity. Kadir had popped more than one lame niggah who thought he could beat him outta what was rightfully his. These two white boys would be no fuckin' exception.

He was enjoying himself though. Like a cat, he played with his prey a little bit before he snuffed them. Big Boy was cryin' and pissin' and Kadir wanted to see what else he would do. He'd test the limits of his manhood. There was no way to predict what a man would do when he knew he was facing certain death. Some dudes got brave, like the short cat with the blond hair. They accepted death with courage and faced that shit square on. Others, like Big Boy, pissed up their clothes and begged. Kadir cocked his gun. He liked it when they begged.

Right on cue, Big Boy started blabbing.

"W-w-wait! Kadir! I got you, man. I'm telling you, I got you!"

Kadir laughed. "Oh you got me, huh? How you figure that, motherfucker? You holding my money in one of your pissy pants pockets or something? 'Cause that's the only way you got me, muhfuckah!"

"I can get it!" His face was red and tears rolled down his cheeks. "I swear on my mother, I can get it!"

Kadir listened.

"My uncle brings in trucks at a warehouse. Sometimes shit falls off the back of them and lands in my garage. He's expecting a shipment from the big guys in North Jersey. Guns. All clean. Squeaky fuckin' clean. I can hook you up, dude, give you a whole crate. Make that two fuckin' crates! For real, I—"

Kadir laughed. Who the fuck did he look like? Was he supposed to go out there and fence off some stolen Mafia guns to get back his own money?

"Man, you must be stu—"

His cell phone vibrated. With his gat still trained on the two cowering white boys, Kadir reached for his phone without glancing down.

"What it do?"

He listened for a moment, his mind going numb. Farad's voice was low and deadly on the other line, and the information he relayed was enough to make Kadir start popping off his pistol right then and there.

"What about them Santos dudes?" he asked, his eyes never leaving the cats who were staring into the business end of his gun.

"Yeah. You know that. Some big shit too. Aiight. I'm there, baby. Y'all hold it tight till I get there."

He stuck the phone in his pocket and stepped toward the two young men. Big Boy turned his body sideways and ducked his head, like he could see the bullet coming.

"Y'all muthafuckahs just got saved by the phone." He swung the gun toward Big Boy. "When's that shipment coming in?"

"Tomorrow night. Late. Maybe eleven, but no later than midnight."

Kadir nodded. "I tell you what. I like you. Both of y'all. So I tell you what I'm gonna do." He trained the piece on the short guy, the one who was scared but not a coward. "You been betting high for a long time, so I'ma come to your house first," Kadir told him. "And I'ma pop your woman, right in front of your kids. Then

I'ma take your babies down. One by one. While you watch. Next, I'll find your moms. She's gonna get it bad too, but I respect old people, so I'ma do her kinda quick. But not until I explain this whole thing to her so she knows just how bad you fucked up this time."

Kadir was satisfied by the look on the dude's face. He mighta been brave, but he wasn't a fool. "Then I'm coming for you, Big Boy. But by that time I'll probably be pissed off. Don't count on me to treat your people proper, homey. I get stupid sometimes too, you know. Especially behind my money."

Ten minutes later Kadir was alone in the warehouse, his prey having scurried away with the promised assurances to deliver a package to a designated location in Brooklyn the next night.

Kadir waited until they were gone, then jumped behind the wheel of his Lexus coupe and headed north. His mind wasn't on them low-level cats and it wasn't on no money either. The only thing he could see in front of him was about 70 miles of bad road. Road he was about to burn rubber on so he could get back to his moms's crib and join his brothers as they tried to figure out how to get Baby Brother outta jail.

CHAPTER 4

There's no such thing as a Monster. There's no such thing as a Monster.

Priest awakened to the sound of footsteps outside his door. *There's no such thing as a Monster. There's no such thing as a Monster.* He'd been having a nightmare. The same one he fought against almost every night. The footsteps outside his door were heavy. Different from those made by Finesse or Farad.

There's no such thing as a Monster. There's no such thing as a Monster.

The years he'd spent behind bars had sharpened his senses. Survival had been paramount, especially for a killer like him. Watching his back had been a full-time job, and he was on alert at all times, even when he was asleep or in prayer.

He heard a hand fall on his doorknob and watched it turn. There was no fear in him, but his eyes were trained and his body tensed. He slid his hand under his pillow and searched. Years earlier, his fingers would have come out clutching a burner. Tonight they came out clutching a cross.

There's no such thing as a Monster. There's no such thing as a Monster.

The door opened and light from the hallway spilled into the room. Priest sat partway up and squinted, confused by the sight of his brother standing before him in his uniform.

"What you doing here, Malik? What's going on?"

"Baby Brother," Malik said simply, and Priest fell back against his pillows, the name of his Savior flying from his lips. He felt damnation running through his blood. The sensation of being led to the heights of a mountaintop, only to be hurled over the edge before setting eyes on the glory. *Please,* he prayed. *Don't let that boy suffer for the ills of his brothers.* Oh, God was vengeful.

His strong voice came out in a pained squeak.

"Hurt? Dead?"

Malik shook his head no. "But Sari is."

Relief flowed through Priest and perspiration soaked his bedsheets.

And then came the fear.

"What happened? Where is he? What happened to Sari?"

The answer to those questions hit Priest so low that he rolled over and staggered from the bed. He tripped over his shoes and pushed past Malik to the bathroom, then stood over the toilet and retched. *O, Father, please,* he implored. *Don't let this be true.*

Baby Brother was pure, but every foul thing Priest had ever done flashed through his mind as Malik pulled him to his feet and held him.

"Where they got him at, man?" he begged his younger brother. "We gotta go down there and get him!"

His heart thudded as Malik shook his head with tears in his eyes.

"I already tried, Twan. He had a hearing. You shoulda seen me, man. On my fuckin' hands and knees. I begged that motherfuckin' white judge to release him to me. Told him I'd hold Baby Brother's hand twenty-four seven. I put my badge on that shit. My word. My rep, my whole life!

"That smug bastard refused. He wouldn't even listen when I tried to tell him about Stanford. About the fuckin' scholarship! They don't give a damn about us man. None of us. We just animals locked down in their fuckin' zoos. They charged Baby Brother and threw him back in the bull pen. Told me if I didn't get the fuck outta there, cop or no, I'd be locked in that pen with him."

Priest covered his face with his hands. He knew all too well how quickly things could go wrong in life. For months they'd been waiting for this day. Ever since they'd gotten that scholarship letter they'd been anticipating the joy of lifting Baby Brother from the belly of their Brownsville beast and flying him off to college to pursue his dreams. For the first time since he could remember, Priest mourned for his dead father. For the comfort of having a male figurehead in his life. But he was the top man of the Davis clan. He was the go-to guy, the one everybody looked to for direction when life got hard.

"Then we gotta get him a lawyer," he said, coming to a quick decision. Farad and Finesse had plenty of money. Who cared where they'd gotten it from if it meant Baby Brother might be freed? The Lord forgives! "First thing in the morning, we gotta get Baby Brother a lawyer."

— — — —

Lissa was a skank freak from Harlem, but she gave some damn good brain. Her people owned a time-share up in the Poconos, and even though Raheem knew she was a hoe, the prospect of a long weekend getting his nuts sucked dry was enough to make him agree to drive her up there for Labor Day.

Raheem worked corrections at Rikers Island, and a couple of the C.O.s were from Harlem and had already gotten with Lissa. When they found out he was going to the Poconos for the weekend with a jump-off they tried to fuck with his head, but he just laughed it off. Most of them cats were married. If it wasn't for their wives, any one of them woulda loved to get topped off all weekend long by a wet-neck like Lissa.

It was their last morning and Raheem wanted to make it count. They had been chilling and doing the wild thang up in the mountains for three days and Raheem's tank was just about empty. He'd turned his cell phone off the moment they arrived. Fuck the Department of Corrections this weekend. If anybody called in sick or failed to show up for their shift, he sure hated it for them. They'd have to find some other sucker to come in on a dime because he wasn't leaving these woods until the weekend was over and his balls were turned inside out.

Lissa had treated him to breakfast this morning at a restaurant nearby, and then they'd come back to the room to pack. He'd turned his cell phone back on, placed their bags at the door, then jumped in the shower with Lissa and rubbed soap all over her back. They had planned to leave at noon because of traffic, and that gave Raheem almost two good hours to get his dick wet one last time.

They had just sipped some Krug and he was sitting in a chair rubbing his nuts. Lissa was standing on the bed doing a fat girl's version of a pole dance. She had big titties, but they were floppy and manly looking, just like her shoulders. Her ass was pancake flat with a tattoo on it that said "Jiggly." The skin around her stomach sagged and was covered in crazy stretch marks. But that throat. Goddamn! What a throat! Who needed a round ass and firm tits when they could "Hoover" a niggah's joint the way she did? Just thinking about her lips had Raheem's dick on brick.

Lissa wrapped her fat thigh around one of the bedposts and wiggled her ass suggestively. She had on a baby blue T-shirt with a matching thong, and the fat rolls around her middle tore that thong string up, practically making it disappear.

But that was cool with Raheem. He'd known her body was fucked up when he brought her up here. Let her dance. Just as long as she ended her performance gargling his dick with his balls puffing out both of her cheeks, he was cool.

Lissa slid off the bed and pranced over to where he was sitting. For a freak who pecked wood the way she did, it surprised Raheem that she'd given up on her demand that he go south on her. On the truth tip, he was a true sixty-niner to the bone, but he'd made it clear to Lissa from the gate that he wasn't going out like that with her. She could bounce on his dick, cream all over his fingers. . . . Shit. He'd do just about anything she wanted, but putting his mouth on a nasty freak like Lissa was outta the damn question.

"Yeah, that's right," he growled as she fell to her knees in front of him. "Assume the position, baby. You know how Poppa like his shit done."

He urged her head toward his stiffening dick, but Lissa resisted.

"You a selfish muthafuckah, Raheem! What about how *I* wanna get done? Shit, my fuckin' knees is sore. I'm starting to think the only reason you brought me up here is to get your dick sucked all day long!"

Raheem laughed. "Ya think? Come on, baby. We gotta get outta here in a few hours. Let's finish this party up right, please?"

"No." She crossed her arms and stared at him. "I want you to fuck me."

"Okay." He nodded. "Just gimme a little brain first, sugar. Suck it for a minute, and then we can fuck."

"Hell no. You been tricking me like that all weekend. It's been the same old shit over and over again. I buy the liquor and you get tips. Next thing you know, your ass is horny and you want some head. You tell me to suck it just for a few minutes and end up busting just like that. Then that alcohol hits you and I gotta wait like five hours before your shit gets right again." She rolled her eyes and smirked. "You a piper and everything, Raheem, but I ain't got five hours to wait this morning, baby. I wanna get my sticky off right now, niggah. Not when your shit is half-limp and you can't do nothing with it."

Raheem thought that shit sounded real foul. So what if it was true. The only reason he had agreed to waste a whole weekend on her was for the bomb head she put down. The thought that he wouldn't get to feel them tight lips vibrating on his tip no more scared him. Two minutes later he had her legs in the air, cracking his back in her.

He'd knock her nasty but he wasn't gonna cum. He

was saving his nut for that throat of hers. Lissa moaned and screamed as he dug her belly out. He was a piper all right. Lissa loved it too. She scratched his arms and back and came over and over, screaming out his name. Raheem kept right on pounding, cupping her ass and giving her her money's worth.

She was thrashing around hard, meowing like a cat and shuddering with convulsions. He'd given it to her good, and now it was his turn. He couldn't wait for her to catch her breath so she could put her lip pump on him. He pulled out of her and snatched off his condom, then crawled on his knees until his ass was positioned over her chin. He guided his throbbing head toward her lips, rubbing it all over them so they could get his party started. Lissa sighed and opened her eyes. She smiled and licked her lips. She had just started doing that fantastic thing that no other bitch in the world could do—when the phone rang.

Fifteen minutes later Raheem was heading to the freeway with the rest of the holiday traffic. Every damn body in the world was trying to get back down to the city, and pain ached in him so deeply he had to force himself to take short breaths.

They had his brother. His fuckin' baby brother. On The Rock. Raheem shook his head, trying to clear the picture he saw formulating in his mind. He worked those tiers out on Rikers Island. He knew how shit went down. The mentality of them criminal niggahs. Fuck! He shoulda never turned off his phone. Malik said they'd been trying to catch him since early Sunday morning, and here it was Monday already. Baby Brother had been on Rikers for over twenty-four fuckin' hours and he hadn't known about it. Raheem cursed under his breath. Them niggahs on The Rock was grimy as fuck. He couldn't even see Baby Brother dwelling next to that slime element.

Raheem was running on pure adrenaline. He had dragged Lissa outta the room and threw their bags in the back of his ride. Gunning his motor, he'd squealed out of the parking lot and zipped down the streets toward the highway.

"You gonna tell me what the big emergency is?" Lissa had stunted, sliding across the seat as he made a sharp turn and ran a red light.

"Bitch," Raheem said, his voice burning the air like

fire. "Shut the fuck up. Don't you open your mouth no more until you outta my ride."

Evil was upon him and Raheem knew it. The last time he'd felt this way was when Antwan had gotten in that trouble up in Greenhaven. Of all the Davis brothers, Raheem's temper was the most uncontrollable. Baby Brother was the best of the bunch, no doubt. But while Antwan had found God, Kadir was a master gambler, the twins were ruthless drug lords terrorizing niggahs on the streets, and Malik was a cop who loved the whole world, there had always been a storm brewing in Raheem. He hid it well, though. He wasn't about to jeopardize his standing in the Department of Corrections by strangling every mothafuckah who pissed him off. The streets of Brooklyn might have hardened him, but repercussions and a responsible job had helped mellow him out. Raheem had learned to control his anger, but underneath his professional demeanor he was cold and brutal, especially when it came to standing on point for his brothers.

But by the time he ejected Lissa's stank ass out on the curb near her apartment and skipped over to Queens to cross the bridge to Rikers Island, there was no fighting the dread he was feeling. He'd replayed

Farad's words in his mind over and over, trying to fit the pieces of the puzzle together. Farad was right. They had to find Sari's killer or shit was gonna spark off in a major way. Them Puerto Ricans loved their blood just like the Davis crew loved theirs. Tony Santos was gonna bring war down and send blood running in the gutters, and somebody was gonna get fuckin' hurt.

Raheem gripped the steering wheel and stood up on the gas pedal. It wasn't even a fuckin' possibility that Baby Brother had killed nobody. Especially his girl, Sari. His brother was a hard-body mothafuckah. A solid little niggah. He could handle any niggah on the streets and even them slime-buckets on the tier if he had to. But he wasn't a killer. Every ounce of the Davis hope was riding on Baby Brother's shoulders. They were depending on him to create the kind of life for himself that the rest of them hadn't been able to manage.

Raheem parked in the employee lot and ran toward the entrance. He nodded at a few C.O.s who were standing around talking, and headed over to the reception center. No matter how much he tried to fight off that rising feeling that signaled impending dread and doom, he just couldn't shake it.

"Chill the fuck out, niggah," he scolded himself.

"B-Brother is tight. That niggah prolly chillin' and maintaining his space right now."

But Raheem was wrong.

Because as it turned out, it didn't matter how much rubber he burned on the road, or how much he tried to fill his own head with positive hype. Yeah, Baby Brother was fearless, just like his brothers. He was a fighter who had come up in the streets and knew how to annihilate a mothafuckah with his bare hands. But none of that shit meant a damn thing by the time Raheem ran across the grounds and pushed through the door of the Otis Bantam Center. Because time hadn't stood still waiting for him to come down from the Poconos. The clock had kept right on ticking while Raheem was out there chasing him a dick-licking, and by the time he found somebody to tell him where his baby brother was, it was already too late.

CHAPTER 5

Life was moving fast for Baby Brother in the joint. *Strip naked, bend over, spread your cheeks.* He did all that and more. He went through the motions like a man made of stone. Not a hint of emotion flickered on his face. He was attuned to his surroundings, but cold and unfeeling inside.

He refused to think about Sari. He pushed the image of her bloody body deep into the recesses of his mind where it couldn't hurt him. He wouldn't let it weaken him neither. He'd come of age in an area of Brooklyn where the criminals crawled real low in the gutta. A project-trained niggah like him knew survival in the joint was a day-by-day thing. He'd seen what prison had done to Antwan. How his brother had been churned and burned by the acidic shit floating around in the belly of this same beast. Rikers might not have been as high-post as Comsackie or Greenhaven, but this is where them upstate niggahs got their start. Some of the most ruthless and despicable criminals in the city were behind these walls. Baby Brother put himself into a state of mind that was similar to a boxer's zone. He was like a coiled snake. On guard and ready to strike.

Malik had shown up while he was still locked down in a bull pen at Central Booking. The judge had just denied Malik's request to release him into his care. It had fucked Baby Brother up to hear Malik begging that white mothafuckah like that. Malik had poured out everything in his heart as he made his impassioned plea on Baby Brother's behalf, telling the court all about Stanford and the prestigious full scholarship that Baby Brother had earned.

"Your Honor," Malik had said. "My fellow officers have arrested the wrong man. My little brother is innocent. He's going to college. To Stanford University in California!" He'd turned and looked into Baby Brother's eyes. "He's gonna be a surgeon. A baby surgeon. Everything he's ever done in life was to help other people, and to make our dead mother proud."

But the judge had given less than a fuck about Baby Brother's accomplishments. That shriveled up mothafuckah had actually yawned while Malik damn near sank to his knees pleading for his understanding and mercy.

Baby Brother had gone even colder inside. He'd tried his best to make good decisions and do the right thing his whole life. Most of the shit other young heads in the hood indulged in, he had sworn he would avoid. There had been no rock-slanging, no wild fucking, no all-night drinking. Baby Brother had never jacked nobody for their car or knocked a bird on her ass. For the first time in his life he was on the opposite end of a good thing, and seeing Malik have to beg a motherfuckah like that infuriated him.

"Raise up . . ." Baby Brother had muttered under his breath from the bench he was chained to. Malik was bent with pain. "Don't you beg that mothafuckah for me. . . ."

After the hearing when Malik came back to the bull pen, they'd given up the dap, then his brother had pulled him close and held him briefly. Baby Brother picked up the scent of fear on his brother and he knew why. A cop's brother was a target in the joint. Malik mighta been Mr. Personable, but he was still the po-po, and as such he still had enemies.

"Stay strong, Baby Brother. We'll figure something out, yo. All of us are working on this, night and day."

Baby Brother had nodded and backed away from his brother. He was the youngest of the crew, yeah. But he was just as hard as the rest of his brothers. He'd hang until they got him out. He'd fend, he'd fight, he'd do whatever the fuck he had to do. He'd survive.

CHAPTER 6

But it wasn't any of Malik's enemies that shoulda concerned Baby Brother. The correctional facilities at Rikers were supposed to be less intense than the stone-walled prisons in upstate New York, but you couldn't tell it by the grimy shit that went down on The Rock. Every new inmate in the place wanted to take a hard rep with them when they got transferred up north. If they were vicious enough on Rikers Island, then their name would precede them and their problems would be fewer when they got up there to the real doghouse.

As Baby Brother was led down the hall he passed between a row of cells where inmates grasped the bars and checked out the new meat. He walked like the niggah he was. Upright. Confident. He didn't grill nobody, but he didn't avoid nobody neither. Shit was talked on either side of him, but that was to be expected. He didn't take it personally because these niggahs didn't know him.

At least he didn't think they did.

"Yo, Acqui!" a short, powerfully built dude named

Rayz called out to his man on the other side. They were both down with the Brooklyn Borne click and had gotten knocked a couple of weeks earlier for kicking down the door of a state witness's house and tying up the man and his whole family before pouring lighter fluid on them and setting the house on fire.

"I know that cat, son. He looks real familiar. . . . Look at them eyes. That's that niggah Farad's brother, yo! One of them Davis dudes." His hand went to the spot where his right ear had once been. "Yo . . . what the fuck that niggah doing up in here?"

Across the way, Acqui frowned. The degradation Farad and Finesse had put him and his boy through had been so severe and humiliating it was like a living thing, never far from his mind. "Oh, he up in here about to get served, that's what the fuck he doin'," he said.

Acqui grinned. A cold breeze seemed to come from his direction. He had been itching to pump lead into Farad and Finesse for a while now. Them niggahs had a tight circle, though, and kept their strap on at all times.

But he would never forget the doggin' they'd put on him. Them niggahs had got him and Rayz in the middle of a crowd of niggahs and bitches and shit on them in the worst possible way.

"Get yo mothafuckin ass over here!" Finesse had demanded, the blade of his knife still dripping with Rayz's blood. They'd been chillin' in a little joint called The Bad Ass. Hoes and dice were being tossed in the back room, and them Davis twins had busted Rayz and Acqui flipping loaded dice.

Rayz had gotten the worst of it. Physically, that is.

"Don't even step toward that fuckin' door!" Finesse had warned Rayz when he tried to dip out the back room. They shouldn'ta had their asses up in there no way. They were from Brownsville, but had gone to Jeff High School back in the day and straddled the line between Brownsville and East New York. But still, even though they were technically still in The Ville, they were way out of Borne territory, and just about every niggah up in there was down with the Davis crew.

Rayz had kept on moving. He was only a few feet away from the door, and he coulda got through that shit too, but a thick-necked niggah named Dolla stepped in front of him and checked the door.

That was all the time Finesse had needed. He crossed the room in four long strides and snatched Rayz up in a headlock. Without saying a word, that mothafuckah yanked out a blade and sliced, and the next thing Acqui knew Finesse was holding up a bloody ear, niggaz was laughin' and wildin', and Rayz was on the floor bleeding from the head and hollerin' like a punched-out old lady.

And then it was Acqui's turn to suffer. The club owner, Jed, kept pit bulls in the back for security purposes. But Farad wasn't satisfied with mutilating Rayz. That niggah wanted to humiliate them too.

"Get on your fuckin' hands and knees!" he had ordered Acqui. "Crawl over there and stick ya face in that fuckin' dog bowl!"

Rage had surged through Acqui, but survival was in him too. Ignoring the jeers from the cats in the crowd and the squeals of disgust coming from the jawns, Acqui doggy-walked across the room to where Farad stood by the three dog bowls. Once there, it was hard to lift his eyes. He was so consumed with killing somebody that his whole body trembled.

"Lap it up, bitch."

Finesse had passed his twin the torch. Farad mighta been quieter than his brother, but he was just as grimy. "Put ya face down and lap up every fuckin' ounce."

Acqui looked down and almost got sick. There was all kinds of shit floating around in them foul-smelling dog bowls. Bits of pit hair, trails of slobber, soggy crumbs of food. And who the fuck knew what else. Tears of fury rose in his eyes and he had to force himself to stay on his knees. His Glock was under the seat of his whip. It didn't matter. Lunging for Farad's throat while he was surrounded by his crew woulda been suicide.

It had taken every ounce of control Acqui had inside to make himself chill. To wait for a better day. And now, watching that black niggah with the unmistakable Davis eyes stroll down the walkway toward an end cell, it looked like the day he'd been waiting for had finally arrived. He headed toward the phones to place a call to his niggah Borne and get permission to put in work.

— — — —

Baby Brother had been assigned to work in the kitchen.

He had only been locked down for a day and didn't think they would give him a job so soon, but he didn't question it. Anything that would keep him outta his shit-smelling cell was cool. It wasn't that he was anxious to get out there with the crazies or nothing, but almost anything was better than sitting up in that tiny-ass jawn with his cellie.

That cat was bugged. Something had happened to him that sent him off the radar. He'd been locked up in reception for three months already and according to the guy in the cell next to theirs, the niggah hadn't washed his ass the whole time.

The stench coming from the cell had almost dropped Baby Brother at the door. His eyes had watered and his stomach turned over. No human being could smell this fuckin' foul, and once he ventured more fully inside the room he saw what the true problem was.

His cellie was a shit-thrower.

Hard clumps of tossed shit stuck to the walls, the floor, and even the ceiling.

"Yo!" Baby Brother wilded out on him. "What the fuck is wrong with you, homey!" All the feelings he had been holding back came rushing out in rage and disbe-lief. "You gonna clean this motherfuckin' shit up, man! How the hell you living? Look, niggah. Take a fuckin' shower. Wash your fuckin' *ass*! And clean this shit up or get fucked up!"

The cat had given Baby Brother a sullen look, then reluctantly began scraping shit off the walls. He pulled some unused cleaning supplies from under his bunk and started cleaning. "You gonna see, man. Just watch. You gonna see. You gotta keep these niggahs offa you some kinda way."

Baby Brother was so mad he couldn't hold still. He paced two steps up and back, trying hard to hold his breath while his cellie slung shitty water around the room with a dirty mop.

He couldn't believe they had put him in with this fool, and when he thought back to when one of the guards called out his cell number, he remembered everybody laughing like that shit was a joke.

It took over three hours before Baby Brother was able to fully enter the room to put his belongings down and make up his bunk. He'd made his cellmate work up a sweat. He had given him directions while he scrubbed the floors, the walls, and the ceiling. Then Baby Brother ordered him to go take a shower.

The young man started trembling.

"A shower?" He looked around the cell and started shifting from one foot to the other nervously. He wiped his face on his sleeve. "I—I—I . . . man, I don't think I can do that."

Baby Brother got swole. He was tired, he was angry, he was locked up, and he was innocent. He was also ready to hurt some fuckin' body.

"Man, I ain't playing with you. You either wash your ass or get took down."

Cellie shrugged. "Do what you gotta do, niggah. I rather get took down than get ass-fucked."

Baby Brother stared at him. This fool was serious. Fear was in his eyes, but it wasn't because Baby Brother had put it there. He was a pretty niggah. Green eyes, wavy hair, dimples and pretty lips. Damn right he was scared. But the thing he feared was much bigger than the eighteen-year-old accused murderer standing in front of him.

Baby Brother put his gear down and got up on his bunk. He stared at the ceiling as his heart pounded and his mind raced. This place was a cesspool. A mother-fuckin' sewer. Niggahs shit on each other up in here all the time. In more ways than one.

He sat alone at lunchtime. The food was grim. Sliced turkey, peas, lumpy potatoes. Baby Brother dug in without looking at it. Survival was paramount and he had to eat to live. He was surprised when an inmate sat down across from him.

"We cool?"

It was Dirtbag, his stank-ass cellie. Fouling up the air. Baby Brother ignored the fool and kept eating.

He was on a mission. He knew his brothers were on the outside working like hell for him. All he had to do was stay cool and mark down the days until they got him out.

"I heard you popped a Puerto Rican chick," his cellie said, his eyes scanning the room. "That means you better watch your back around these P.R. cats in here."

Baby Brother gulped from his carton of milk like his cellie wasn't even there.

"And them mothafuckin Asians is tryna come up too." Dirtball twisted his arm behind him and dug down his shirt, trying to scratch his own back.

"See that dude over there with all the muscles? They call him Doobie. He's down with that notorious 'Kill-A-Man Crew.' Watch them niggahs too. They treacherous on the real."

For the first time Baby Brother acknowledged the fact that Dirtball was even sitting at his table. He looked across the room and damn if it wasn't Doobie. He knew the niggah well and had never liked him. Smooth, slick, and used to run drugs for Farad and Finesse. Without a word, he stood and picked up his tray. Igging Dirtbag, he walked over to the trash and dumped his leavings, then headed out of the dining room.

He was stopped at the door.

"Hey," a corrections officer called out to him. He was standing near the doorway with his arms crossed. Salt-and-pepper hair streaked his temples and Baby Brother figured he was a vet who had been on the job for a while. "They need you in the kitchen right now. Run back there and ask for Dreamer. He's your new boss. He'll tell you what you need to do."

The kitchen was industrial-sized. It was bigger and more complex than any Baby Brother had ever seen. Inmates were doing all sorts of chores. From cutting vegetables to boiling huge vats of noodles, shit was getting done up in there.

"Over here," the cat named Dreamer directed him. "I'ma put you on the dishwasher team today. I hope you learn quick 'cause we on a strict schedule back here and ain't nobody got time to show you nothing more than once."

Baby Brother shrugged. There were plastic containers filled with dirty plates and utensils waiting to be washed. He shook his head. He'd graduated with a 4.0 grade average. How fuckin' hard could loading up a dishwasher be?

He was working alone, transferring dirty silverware

to the dishwasher rack, when it happened. The first blow caught him in the back of the head, stunning him and propelling him so hard he landed halfway inside the industrial dishwasher.

They hit him behind the knees next, causing him to arch his back and slide to the ground in agony. The entire silverware tray came down with him, and instinctively he closed his hand around a piece of cool metal.

"Yeah!" he heard one of his attackers yell out. "Payback, mothafuckah! It's get-back time!"

Baby Brother tried to stand. Payback? He glanced up and saw five inmates. They were all strangers. Fists flew and boots stomped. They pummeled him everywhere and Baby Brother rolled with the blows as best he could.

The blow to the head had weakened him. Dulled his reflexes. He tried to cover his head and ball up in a knot, and that's when they started dragging him. Three niggahs grabbed his legs and pulled him across the now-deserted kitchen. Workstations had been abandoned, vegetables left unchopped on counters, and huge pots were boiling unwatched.

Baby Brother felt frigid air wash over him and realized that they'd dragged him into the walk-in freezer.

He came alive with a fury. He thrust his heel into a pair of nuts and heard a sickening thunk as he connected. On his feet, he bobbed and weaved, energized like a punch-crazy boxer who had found his second wind.

With the piece of metal still clenched in his hand, Baby Brother lunged at a skinny dude with a big head, stabbing him deeply in the throat with a fork and sending him down for good. He whirled and hit another inmate so hard, his front teeth flew out.

Baby Brother fought like a champion. Two of his attackers were out for the duration, and that left three against one. He gave it just as good as he took it, using every bit of street skills he had and calling up power and endurance from the pit of his soul. He went down quite a few times, but so did his attackers. Blood was everywhere, and all four men were sweating in that freezer.

He swung a hard right and knocked down a short niggah with a long ponytail, then side-kicked the burly cat on his left. But as his foot touched the ground and he prepared to whirl to his right, an industrial-sized black skillet loomed in front of him and a moment later his skull cracked and his world went dark.

Baby Brother came to on his stomach.

He was in a hard yoke, his head locked in the crook of a muscular arm.

Blood dripped from his face and into his eyes, and his whole body was on fire. He was dizzy, suffocating. His pants were yanked down. There was thrusting movement behind him. Probing, and then explosive pain. He gasped as he was penetrated, unable to inhale a full breath.

"Yeah, mothafuckah!" a heavy voice growled in his ear. His muscles were clenched as his manhood was brutally violated. "Who's doin' the dog now, bitch! This for your bitch-ass brothers, son!"

Baby Brother broiled. A rage greater than any he could have imagined exploded from him. He screamed inside and rose up on his arms, bucking his rapist off of him. From his knees, he reached back and felt for the nuts of his choker, seeking to rip them from the man's body.

Blind and choking, he was on one knee and had managed to get one foot planted on the floor, and then it happened.

White heat seared from his left ear all the way across to his right. The air he'd been so desperate to breathe was now totally gone. He gurgled and clutched his bloody throat, and the truth was right there in his hands.

He'd been buck-fiffed.

Smiley-faced. His neck slit from ear to ear.

Baby Brother fell forward, the icy floor no match for the fire in his lungs. His struggle was weak and brief. His death, violent and vicious. His last moments were comforting, though. His life had been cut short, but it had not been without love. For the next sixty-eight seconds Baby Brother lay on a dirty freezer floor gasping and gurgling, drowning in a pool of his own blood. He thought of his parents and of his brothers, and prepared to meet Sari.

CHAPTER 7

aheem was on fire. Outta all the mothafuckahs they coulda played with, they picked him. He had nutted up like a crazy man in the admin office. Them mothafuckas shoulda known better!

"Y'all put my little brother in a cell with Dirtbag? Who the fuck made that goddamn decision?"

The young C.O. on duty raised his hands. "It wasn't me, man. I don't even think nobody knew he was your family, man. If we woulda known, you know we woulda looked out, bruh."

Raheem had tossed the whole damn office up. Slinging chairs, throwing manuals and logs and daring some fuckin' body to try to stop him.

"I'm gone down there to get my brother outta that goddamn cell, you hear? Y'all better put him in Adult Segregation right now. Lock him down and get him away from them fuckin' animals, *right now.* Call whoever you gotta call. I don't care what you gotta do to make that shit happen, but you better do it."

He stormed down the halls heading toward Dirtbag's cell. Even the guards stayed outta that joint. The
cat was harmless, but he was pure slime. He couldn't
even let his mind imagine what his brother must have
faced going up in there.

But as Raheem rounded a corner he saw two C.O.s
standing outside of Dirtbag's cell.

"Yo!" he called out, making his presence known.
"Bring my brother outta there right the fuck now!"

But when he got up closer on the cell he saw that
some sort of investigation was under way.

"I'm sorry, man," an officer named Joplin said. He
was a cool cat from Tilden Houses and had gone to Jeff
High too. His mom had died young and he'd spent a lot
of time in the Davis house with Raheem and Kadir.

He reached out and grabbed both of Raheem's
broad shoulders and hugged him. "Zab is gone, Rah. Shit
got all fucked up in the kitchen. Somebody turned they
fuckin' head and played possum. I'm sorry, man."

"What you saying, Jop?" Raheem pushed away and
searched his friend's eyes, praying he was interpreting
shit wrong. "What you mean, man?"

"They caught Baby Brother on kitchen duty, Rah.
Buck-fiffed."

The blood froze in Raheem's veins. He staggered and went down to one knee, all six feet five inches of brawn and muscle now a big blob of grief-stricken jelly.

His brother was dead and he felt responsible. If he hadn't switched shifts he woulda been there when they brought Baby Brother in. He could have protected him. Got him in Adult Segregation and kept him safe. Raheem cried. He didn't give a fuck about the inmates who watched through the bars as he grieved on the floor. His baby brother was dead. The hope of his family was gone. How was he gonna go home and tell his other brothers some shit like that?

"Where is he?" he demanded, rising to his feet and looking around wildly. "Where the fuck they took my brother, man?" he demanded from Joplin and the other guards. "Some fuckin' body better show me where the fuck my baby brother is right the fuck now!"

They saw the craziness in him and ten minutes later Raheem was standing in the prison morgue. He didn't know the cat who worked down there, but his Corrections ID and the rage in his eyes was enough to convince the dude that Baby Brother was his family member.

"You know I'm supposed to wait until the family is officially notified, then do the whole identification process with a photo. You sure you up for this?"

Raheem had nodded yes, but when the morgue tech pulled the sheet back and he saw the brutality that had been inflicted on his younger brother, his knees sagged and he nearly stopped breathing as he grasped the cold metal gurney for support.

"Oh shit," he cried, reaching out for Baby Brother's cool body. Raheem slid his arm under his brother's head and pulled him close, hot tears falling from his eyes as he moaned out loud, rocking the corpse and consumed with grief.

The tech stood by silently for a moment, then turned away, allowing his fellow officer a moment of grief. But Raheem was oblivious to everything except the fact that his brother was gone and that he hadn't been there to save him.

Mama! he cried inside, his soul filled with shame. *We was supposed to watch him, Mama! You begged us to look out for him. To take care of him! I'm sorry, Mama. Please . . . forgive me . . . I'm so sorry!*

— — — —

Two days later the Davis boys were mourning the murder of their beloved brother and plotting their revenge. The Santos family had already buried Sari, and Tony had gone off the deep end, terrorizing fools in broad daylight. Promising to rearrange some faces, his goonies were wreaking havoc in East New York and tossing anybody he even thought mighta been holding out on information into the Gowanus Canal.

Farad and Finesse had their crew out there too. Baby Brother had been murdered on The Rock, but they knew the streets still demanded a reckoning and they were both ready to get shit popping.

"It's go to muthafuckin' war time," Finesse announced. Rage was in the air as they sat at their mother's dining room table. "Somebody gotta pay for this shit, yo. The blade mighta been pulled from inside the joint, but the order came from outside the walls. My cats are out the streets with their ears close to the ground. A name is gonna fall outta somebody's mouth before you know it. And when it does, we gone light these mothafuckin streets up with bullets and blood!"

Farad agreed. "Yeah. Any minute now," he said, then nodded toward his brother Raheem, who sat with his elbows on the table and his face in his hands. "You still got them snitches behind the walls, right?"

Raheem looked up. "Yeah. I'm leaning hard on Baby Brother's cellie. That dirty bastard knows something and he's gonna tell it. I think it mighta been that niggah whose nose I cracked last year. The one who tried to bite me."

"Could be, but I been hearing noise about that fool Borne," Finesse said. "He was breakin' some of his new boys in the night Sari got popped. They was in the right area, son. And one of them cats dry-snitched and wrote a letter to his girl telling her somebody took down a Puerto Rican chick."

Malik shook his head and crossed his arms. As a police officer he'd seen all kinds of shit on the streets. Black-on-black crime was ridiculous. It was the cheapest and most efficient method available for the white man to get rid of his problems. "I know for a fact Borne's kids gotta slump somebody before they can get a tat and roll with him. And most of them be real young heads too. We've brought him in for contributing to the delinquency of a minor quite a few times, but he always manages to beat that shit."

"But where was the fuckin' C.O. who shoulda been holding down the kitchen!" Kadir demanded. He had made it in from A.C. and had been planning to ride with

Antwan to visit Baby Brother as soon as Raheem gave them the word.

"Oh," Raheem said quietly as a dark cloud came across his face, "don't worry about that niggah. I'ma handle that. When I'm finished with that slime his bitch and kids ain't even gonna recognize him."

Priest sat at the head of the table with his hands clasped in front of him, praying quietly. He'd had to chase their dun-duns away from the front door, off of the stoop. They didn't need no security, he explained. Baby Brother was gone, and now all they needed was the love of God and the strength to make it through.

He'd come inside and sat listening while his brothers vented, letting them talk their grief out. All of them had bloody hands. Farad and Finesse sold drugs, but they'd killed whenever the need arose.

And Malik. As happy as that cat was, he was still a black man with a gun. A couple of years back there'd been an Internal Affairs investigation that implicated him in some dirty business involving one of the top detectives in his precinct. Somebody had shot a young white man who was supposedly slumming through Brownsville to purchase drugs. The murder weapon was never found, but witnesses put Malik and the detective on the scene, although both of them denied any involvement.

Kadir was wild, like their father. He lived a dangerous life down in Atlantic City and probably had more bodies floating in the ocean than he'd ever admit. But Raheem . . . Antwan knew his brother like the back of his own hand. He walked a straight line when he could, but he was the most ruthless of them all when crossed.

"Leave it alone, Raheem. We gonna leave the retribution for the Lord, remember?"

Raheem snorted. "You the one preachin', Antwan. Not me. I ain't worried about my fuckin' soul. All I'm worried about is not getting mines."

"That's what's real," Farad said, staring coldly at his oldest brother. "I can't believe you so stuck on that Jesus shit that you would let a niggah murk your fuckin' brother and tell us to leave the get-back for the Lord. You soft as fuck these days, man."

Priest held up his hand. "Don't roll out on me too far," he warned sternly. "Everybody just chill out and let's concentrate on getting Baby Brother in the ground. He didn't live no life of crime, and we ain't gonna blacken his memory with none either. All this payback and get-back y'all talking ain't gonna do nothing to bring him back. This thing could get bigger and uglier and the only thing that'll accomplish is the spilling of more blood. Besides"—he glared at Farad and Finesse—"both of y'all out on parole as it is. You wanna go back upstate and get tossed in the bing like I did? Didn't I do enough hard time for all of us?" He shook his head and glared at each of his brothers, letting them know that despite the priest's collar he wore around his neck, he was still large and in charge.

"Now I said what I said, and I meant it. It's final. Let the cops handle it. That's what they get paid to do. Malik's gonna have his boys all over it. They'll make sure justice gets served."

Raheem spoke quietly. His eyes were red and full of tears. "Those slime-bags *banged* him, Antwan! They stuck their dicks up his ass, then cut his fuckin' throat. Now you might be able to close your eyes and not see that shit. You might be able to search your soul and not feel it too. *But I can't.*"

Priest tightened his muscles, absorbing his brother's wrath deep in his soul. He knew all about prison rapes. He had groveled around like a dog behind those bars before God took mercy and spoke to him.

He'd participated in acts so grimy that no amount of baptism could wash the stink of his deeds from his spirit. *There's no such thing as a MONSTER. There's no such thing as a MONSTER. There's no such thing as a MONSTER.* But still. He'd been blind then. Just a snake crawling around on its belly in the darkness. He was trying to live a redeemed life now, and the retaliation his brothers were suggesting was sinful.

"I said, leave it be. All of us need to take a page outta Baby Brother's book. The way he lived his life should be an example to us. Let's not use his death as an excuse to do even more wrong in our lives. As hard as it might be, and bad as it might hurt, we gonna do this the *right* way. Leave Borne and his crew alone. Whatever them fools got coming, they'll get it. Now leave it alone."

‑‑ ‑‑ ‑‑ ‑‑

Five nights later Priest was feeling low. Baby Brother had been buried, and the stress of going through the emotional, jam-packed funeral and keeping his younger brothers in check at the same time had taken a physical toll on him, and his body was in turmoil.

"I'm going out to get some juice," he told Farad,

rubbing his throat. Finesse was upstairs in bed with a girl, Kadir was on the road back to Atlantic City, and Malik and Raheem had just gone back to the house they shared in Crown Heights.

Sitting at the table, Farad looked up as his brother dragged out the door. Antwan looked bad. Worn. The funeral had hit them all hard, especially since Baby Brother's coffin had been closed, a telltale sign of his brutal and disfiguring death. But Priest had taken it hardest. He was the oldest and used to be the baddest and the meanest. He was the protector of his clan. Mother and father to his younger brothers, and he took it as if their failure to protect Baby Brother rested squarely on his shoulders.

Priest ambled down the streets of Brooklyn with his mother on his mind. She had been such a beautiful woman. Tall, well-shaped, with the most amazing dark-chocolate skin and a dazzling smile. Their father had been muscular and very light-skinned, with amber eyes, which was the only physical attribute he had passed on to any of his sons.

It was late, but his throat was sore and he needed relief, as well as a little solitude. He walked through the doors of the Key Foods supermarket and headed straight for the refrigerated section along the back row of the store. He selected a quart of Tropicana in a smooth glass jar, then stopped in the medicine aisle and picked up a box of Sucrets.

There was only one cashier open, but the line was pretty short. Priest stood behind a group of young thugs who were cutting up. Their whole demeanor reflected drug involvement, hood life, and street culture. They were loud and abrasive. Profanity-laced tirades spilled from their mouths and echoed throughout the store.

Priest stared at them. At their clothing, their jewelry, and the cases of beer and bottles of alcohol they carried in each hand. They were a reflection of his younger self. A milder reflection, true, but if they committed enough crimes and crawled in the gutters long enough, they might be able to get half as grimy as he'd been.

"Man, I'm 'bout to get me some pussy!" one of the young heads said, balancing his case of brew against the counter and rubbing his dick with his free hand. He was tall and light, solidly built with a shiny bald head. "I ain't had a bitch since I got outta Rikers!"

His boy looked at him and laughed. "Niggah, you been on the streets for two days and you ain't got a piece of ass yet?"

One of the others, a short yellow kid with a long ponytail laughed even louder. "He said pussy, niggah! He got him a piece of ass in the joint, man!"

The bald-headed cat shrugged. "Yeah. I had to grin a niggah last week, yo. I'on't be playing with dudes, ya know?"

"Oh, man! Y'all shoulda seen that cat!" the short kid hollered. "That motherfuckah fought like hell! Stabbed my man Rant in the neck with a fuckin' fork! Took him out! That was Borne's lil cousin, yo! We ended up dragging that fool in the meat locker. I slammed him over the head with a frying pan, then Qui put that niggah in a throat-lock and dicked him!"

Shorty with the lemon face laughed hysterically.

"Y'all shoulda seen how that niggah bucked Qui off! My niggah had to deep smiley him to get him to lay down. Blood was running all outta that black fool. From his throat *and* his ass!"

Priest staggered, losing his grip on the orange juice. The bottle hit the floor and exploded, sending yellow liquid mixed with glass shards all across the dirty linoleum.

"What the fuck!" a brown-skinned youth in a red-and-yellow shirt turned around and hollered as the liquid splashed the back of his pant legs and his Ice Cream sneakers by Pharrell.

"Yo, you stupid mothafuckah! What the hell is wrong with you, man?" He stepped up on Priest, embarrassed and swollen with anger. "Preacher or no preacher, I oughta fuck yo ass up!"

Baby Brother, Priest raged inside, the graphic description of his brother's murder ringing in his ears. They talked about it like his baby brother wasn't shit. Like he didn't have no purpose in this world, like didn't nobody love him. No longer were his brother's killers just some random inmates in a depraved criminal justice system. They had faces. Bodies. Their confession was in the air burning his ears. The brutal pictures Priest had tried so hard not to see were now permanently etched in his mind. His blood was full of ice as the young cat beefed in his face. *There's no such thing as a MONSTER. There's no such thing as a MONSTER. There's no such thing . . .*

Priest just stood there as the youngster based and his boys yeasted him up, encouraging him to action. He took the threats in silence. He was battling for his soul and he couldn't even speak. There was a time when he would have bitten every last one of them. Bitten all of them at the same time. Buried their punk asses where they stood. Sent their mamas scurrying downtown to make funeral arrangements. But all he could do now was stare into their faces as he slammed his grief down and fought the monster-sized fury that was trying to take its place.

He got a good look at them. At all of them. But especially at the tall dude they'd called "Qui." This young niggah had bought and paid for whatever retribution ended up coming to him. He'd earned his wrath, cash and carry. Priest dropped his Sucrets to the ground and began walking away, his eyes recording their features like a video camera. That dude Acqui was in trouble.

Storming back down the wet streets with deliberate purpose, Priest went into criminal-minded mode as Antwan "Monster" Davis, that brutal killer he had convinced himself was dead, emerged and took over the show, bigger and badder than ever. There was work to be done. Retribution to be exacted. Bodies to be buried. By the time he burst through his front door he was fully transformed, with nothing but crushing bone and spilling blood on his mind.

"Whattup?" Farad asked as the front door flung open, then slammed violently shut. He whirled around in his chair and was shocked by what he saw. *Damn. Whattup, stranger?* It had been a long time since this cat had menaced the streets of Brooklyn. For the longest time Farad had wondered if he would ever see him again.

"Uh-oh," he said as the familiar stranger moved toward their mother's kitchen table. Deadly. Brutal. Swollen with fury.

"Monster's back."

CHAPTER 8

Finesse burnt up the phone lines.

"Yo, Leek. Y'all at the crib yet? Oh, y'all swung by White Castle? Well snatch Rah outta the muh-fuckin line and y'all circle back to the crib, man! Hell yeah I'm serious. Nah, I ain't got no new info! I got something better than that, baby. Yeah, my niggah. We got us a Monster breaking shit up in this joint again, man, and he's calling for a meeting."

Two minutes later he had Kadir on the line. "Check it out, bruh. You on the Pike? The Garden State? Don't matter, son. Dip at the next exit and turn that whip around. That's right. Head back in, baby. We got some work to put in, homes. A Monster busted up in the crib tonight, man, and he's hungry as hell."

An hour later they sat around their mother's dining room table holding court. The Monster was wearing a red and white Phat Farm shirt and a pair of jeans.

"Farad was right. It was Borne and his niggahs," he told them quietly. His voice was calm, but each of his brothers could see the fury bubbling just under the surface of his skin. It ran up and down the side of his face, his veins throbbing. It was squeezed in his clenched fists and lurked madly just behind his eyes.

"He had his boys out there playing them initiation games. His kid blasted Sari, then let Baby Brother take the fall."

The Monster looked around the table and saw identical rage in five pairs of eyes.

"But Borne's hand is on this shit even deeper than that. Those was his goonies on Rikers too. He cosigned that shit." He glanced at Raheem, who sat there tense and pantherlike. "They back out on the streets now, but they killed Baby Brother for some get-back. I heard 'em say something about crawling on the floor and drinking out of a dog bowl."

Farad was on his feet. He looked at his twin and cursed. "I knew I shoulda popped that bitch niggah when I had him in my crosshairs! That fool don't know fuckin' get-back! I'ma kill him, man!" Tears of frustration were in his eyes as he battled his guilt. Baby Brother had had his throat cut by some come-up niggah. A coward who couldn't even handle his on the street. "I swear, I'ma kill him!"

The brothers stayed in a huddle for most of the

night. They came up with a master plan, scratched it, argued, got mad, came up with something better, refined it, killed certain aspects and agreed on certain others. In the end, their shit was tight and they deferred final judgment to the biggest and the baddest amongst them.

"Good," the Monster growled. "Everybody on point?"

All heads nodded.

Then Farad spoke what was on all their minds. "Yo, I'm down with all this shit we talking about Borne and his crew. I'm on it, sons. But I'ma tell y'all this right now. One of us need to slump that niggah Acqui too. That bitch gotta get smoked."

— — — —

The twins were ready to get shit started. The first thing they did the next morning was roll down Linden Boulevard to sit down with Tony Santos.

"We takin' a bitch?" Farad asked his brother.

Finesse shook his head. "Nah. No burners. No backup neither. Just me and you."

Which could have been a big mistake.

"You steppin up in my crib to confess for your

brother or to drop a dime?" Tony sneered. Sari's death was eating at his bones and he'd sworn the worst kind of vengeance on her killer. He snorted in disgust at the sight of the two tall black men standing before him. Farad and Finesse were fools to roll up in East New York naked. His men were lined up and ready to blast these two niggahs all the way back to Africa. All they needed was the word.

"My brother was innocent," Finesse told him. "And you know that shit. But this ain't no muh'fuckin' dry snitch. This a wet one, homey. Borne Reynolds had ya baby sis popped. He sent his sons out there with orders to take down some Puerto Ricans," he said.

Tony played with his knife. His jaw twitched as his ire churned furiously. As much as he had fucked with Zabu, Tony knew the kid had really dug his sister. Besides, Borne had been encroaching on him in minor ways for a minute now, trying him on the low, annoying him like a gnat. The twins were speaking the truth and Tony knew it. "That fool will never learn," he said finally. "The last time he tried to fuck with me I rearranged his bitch's face. For that he comes after my sister?" He laughed bitterly. "I coulda crumbled his whole house . . . just like that. But I didn't."

"Them the same cats who been breaking into them houses over on Berriman Street too. That old Puerto Rican lady they found strangled a few months back? The one who'd lived in the hood feeding kids for sixty years?" Farad shook his head in disgust. "Who you think raped that old woman? Who choked her? That's one of Borne's too, man! He didn't send nobody out on that shit, though. That's one murder he committed himself."

By the time the twins left East New York, Tony Santos and his Barrio crew had declared war on Borne and his click.

"We got ya back," Finesse had told him as they walked out the door. "Matter fact, gimme twenty-four hours. We got some firepower for you too."

— — — —

Right about this time Kadir was standing in a warehouse watching two white boys pull an assortment of heat out of a stolen Mafia shipment. There were two crates filled with gats. Some were .45's, some were Sigs, a few Glocks, and even a couple of 9mms.

"All of this fall off a damn truck?"

"Nah," the short cat answered. "One was donated

by a friend of mine named Seven. I did a favor for his Get-Money Crew down in Virginia a while back, and he tore me off a few pieces from his stash."

"So are we cool?" the taller of the two asked. The last time Kadir had seen him he was red-faced and scared as fuck, pissing down his own leg.

"Yeah," he told them, eyeing his new arsenal of fire-power. "Almost. Y'all mothafuckas wasn't on time tonight. Two minutes could make the difference between your life or your death. My little package needs a ride, son. A ride to Brooklyn. Handle that shit for me and we'll be straight."

━ ━ ━ ━

Raheem drove into Queens and crossed the bridge to Rikers Island. His mood was pensive, and a hard Reem Raw cut with a gully beat blared from his speakers. Earlier in the day he'd gotten a heads-up from his boy Joppy that he was down on his team. He'd squeezed Dirt-bag and found out which other cats had participated in Baby Brother's murder, and he was ready to help however he could.

They'd met outside Jop's moms' crib, and drank a beer while they tossed info around.

"It was that red niggah Borne," Joplin said, confirming what Raheem and his brothers already knew. "That fool lost control of his sons. He didn't pull no triggers or swing no blades, but them cats belonged to him, so he's responsible."

Raheem nodded, his eyes cold. "What else, Jop? I know you got sumpthin' else for me, man."

"Yeah. I do." He took a long pull from his cigarette and then flicked it into the bushes. "The cat who did Zabu? Him and his man already walked. Zab killed one, but I found out the names of the other two who are still on The Rock. Them fools riding it all the way, though. Dummied up. Don't know shit. But we can get 'em."

That was all Raheem needed to hear. He drove with extreme purpose, going over his plan in his head. He arrived on The Rock and reported for his shift as usual. A couple of his fellow officers had heard about Baby Brother, and they gave their condolences and promised to keep their ears open and let him know what they heard. All inmate deaths were thoroughly investigated, and one of Raheem's boys who worked prison investigations was also down on his team.

"Rah. Don't worry 'bout it, baby. We gonna find out who did that shit. Two inmates got bodied on our watch that day, and we know for a fact there were at least ten inmates in the kitchen who knew what was going down. All them niggahs either went blind or got amnesia, and they swearing to God they don't remember seeing a goddamn thing. But trust. We gonna work it out of 'em."

Raheem had dapped his boy hard and all, but he had no intentions of waiting around for some internal correctional system to exact justice for his brother's life. He was out to get street justice for his. That was truth.

Two hours later Raheem and Joplin were in position and ready to orchestrate their plan. Inmates were constantly being called down to the medical screening room. Sometimes blood tests needed to be run, other times they were asked to update their medical histories. Jop was banging one of the reception center nurses and knew she made a daily run to the other side of the complex for a meeting each Thursday.

He used her computer to send up a request for the two prisoners to report to the nurse's office, then waved Raheem inside and left, closing the door behind him as he walked off whistling down the hall.

Fifteen minutes passed before Raheem heard a knock. He stood behind it with every muscle in his body tensed and ready to spring. It didn't matter who was on the other side of that door, he thought. Whichever one of them niggahs got here first, he was gonna die.

Instead of calling out an answer, he twisted the knob and opened the door, careful to stay hidden behind it. A leg swung forward as the man entered the office, and the moment Raheem saw the fresh sneaker and the telltale prison pants, he swung his right arm in a low roundhouse, catching the inmate by surprise as his prison-made shank sank deeply into the man's belly. His hand moved in a flurry. Once, twice, three times.

"Umph!" was all the niggah said as he clutched his stomach in surprise. Raheem moved swiftly. He grabbed the cat's neck with his left hand and kicked the door shut at the same time. Swinging him around in a yoke, Raheem crushed the inmate's windpipe with his forearm, bending him backward and lifting him off his feet.

"Bitch." He breathed his menace into the struggling man's ear. "That niggah y'all hit in the freezer?" He tightened his grip as the inmate clawed at his arm with one hand and clutched his gutted stomach with the other. "That was a Davis boy, mothafuckah. That was my baby brother."

Raheem pressed the shank into the inmate's temple and pushed hard. The guy would have screamed if he could, but instead his body shuddered for several long moments, and then went still. Raheem's arm trembled as he continued to squeeze the inmate's neck until he was sure there was no life left in him.

A minute later he slung the bloody body to the floor and tossed the shank down beside it. He stood above it looking down in disgust.

One to go.

By the time he heard the next knock at the door he was back in position.

Raheem pulled the door open once again, but this time when the inmate walked in he chilled until the cat was fully in the room. Kicking the door closed, Raheem grabbed the kid from behind. He spun him right, flung him down on top of his dead partner, then landed heavily on top of them both, knocking the air outta the inmate's lungs.

"Yo!" The dude gave a short yell, but Raheem was all over him. He grabbed the inmate's hand and closed it over the shank, crushing his fingers in a vise grip until they closed around the handle. The inmate screamed, both from the pain running up his arm and exploding in his shoulder, and from the sight of his man, dead beneath him on the floor.

Sandwiched between a corpse and a killer, he squirmed and fought, pushing against the warm bloody body as he tried to free his hand from Raheem's deadly grasp.

Raheem grabbed the back of the man's head and smashed his face into the floor, trying to shatter it like an egg. The inmate slumped on top of his friend, down but not out.

"What the fuck are you doing, man?" he whimpered, stretched out helplessly between a rock and a dead man.

"Killing you," Raheem whispered.

Seconds later the door opened and Joppy rushed in.

"Officer down!" he screamed into his walkie-talkie, then jumped on top of the heap as the inmate wiggled weakly beneath them both. "Easy," Joppy cautioned his friend. "Don't go too far, now. We need this mother-fucker alive, man. Ease up now, bruh."

The first three officers responding to the call saw exactly what they were supposed to see: a dangerous, bloody scene. A shanked inmate. And two of their most trusted fellow officers on the ground struggling to restrain an armed killer.

"We got him, fellas." A veteran white officer got on his knees to help. Raheem continued to squeeze the inmate's fist inside his own.

"No! No! No! NO!" the inmate whispered, unable to even move his fingers, let alone escape Raheem's killer clutch.

"Watch the shank!" Raheem shouted. He flailed their arms up and down, back and forth in a mock struggle. "He's still got a shank!"

Minutes later the inmate was restrained and led away and the three officers were standing on their feet, breathing hard and covered in blood.

"We got him," Joplin sighed, clapping Raheem on the back as they waited for the prison investigators to report to the scene. "He won't be hurting nobody no more."

The older white officer wiped his bloody hands on his pants legs and agreed.

"He sure won't. That guy's been through here a few times. He's a three-time felon, you know. That's automatic life."

CHAPTER 9

New York City's drug problem had long been out of hand. Most of the cops who worked narcotics were on the streets undercover, blending into the fabric of the community. Their mission was to infiltrate the various cells that claimed territorial rights all over Brooklyn, and since turnover and burnout were high, much of their success could be attributed to anonymous tips and street informants.

Malik was a down cat on the job. A true brother in blue. A cop's cop. But he also had twin brothers who were deep in the drug game, and he'd come up on the streets with that kind of criminal element.

So when he approached his man Taylor, a brand-new narcotics officer who was bucking hard for a promotion, he knew he'd have very little trouble being persuasive.

"'Sup, Taylor," Malik said, offering the cat some dap. Taylor looked like a damn kid, Malik noticed. He knew Taylor came from one of those rich-niggah families from upstate New York, but the cat had mad street credibility and his swagger and shine came off as truly official.

"Is your boss in, man?" Malik asked the question but he already knew the answer. The head man was at a training conference and wouldn't be back for three days.

Taylor shook his head. "Nah, son. He's outta the office. You can catch him in a couple of days, though."

Malik dapped him like he was ready to walk out, but then shook his head. "That's all right. Shit'll be done jumped off and over with by then, man."

That got him. Taylor was the opportunistic type. Always looking for a leg up the blue ladder. "What's cookin', baby?" he asked, his interest piqued.

"I heard some noise on the streets last night, that's all. A cat I know from back in the day is about to get into some shit, and you know how it be. We on opposite sides of the fence right now, but he still my niggah and I got luh for'im. There's a big drop going down, and a crew of young heads are scheming on some real mutiny shit. My man is in trouble, but he blind and the niggah can't see it. I was gonna whisper a lil something in Big D's ear, but since he ain't here I'ma have to find another way to wrestle this shit."

True to form, Taylor was all ears.

"Dig, man," he said, leading Malik over to a table and pulling out a chair. "Big D don't stop the sun from shining. I got full authorization to act, my man. Ya dude in trouble? Then it's only right that a down cat like you try to help him out."

He waited until Malik was seated, then pulled up a chair beside him.

"So what's poppin, homey? Gimme the who, what, when, and where. I can figure out the why by my damn self."

"Cool," Malik said, sincerity creasing his face. "'Cause I might wear this uniform, yo, but I'm still a street soldier at heart. I luh my niggah Borne, though. I really do. And that's the only reason I'm here, yo. I wanna sink them niggahs plottin' on him, man, because he's a down cat for real, ya know?" He sighed and shook his head. "I'd rather see him locked up in the joint than stretched out in the ground."

The streets were full of danger on Friday nights in Brownsville. The Monster walked down Livonia Avenue on the outskirts of Tilden Projects, where transactions occurred right under the well-lit porches and cats played Cee Low in the lobbies. With eight buildings on the block and sixteen stories in each building, Tilden was like a city within itself. A breeding ground for drugs, crime, and all manner of blight.

He crossed Rockaway Avenue, moving like a hunter as he traveled under the El toward Sutter. Marcus Garvey Houses teemed with criminals and vermin on his left, and Betsey Head Park sat dark and quiet up ahead on his right. He crossed Hopkinson Avenue and walked a few more blocks, then turned the corner on Amboy Street. Minutes later he stood on the raggedy porch of an aged house.

His fist was like a bat as he pounded on the door.

Shuffling feet, a muffled curse. An old woman's voice rang out in the night.

"Who is it?"

He heard the eye-cover slide back and waited until a blurry image appeared at the peephole. He touched his piece to the tiny circle of glass, and then he fired.

On the other side of the door: the sound of a body thumping to the floor, and then another curse. This one much louder.

With his piece aimed, the Monster kicked the door in. It flew wide open, the latch giving way as it slammed inward on its shattered hinges.

An elderly man sitting at a small round table moved toward the kitchen fast, but not fast enough. The Monster stepped over the dead woman and was on him before he knew it. The old man screamed as he fumbled around in a silverware drawer, coming out with a butcher knife. His hand shook. The Monster raged. Laughing, he bent the old man's wrist back, then caught the knife as it fell from his fingers.

The sharp slice of metal moved like a blur. It cut deeply into the withered old flesh: chest, neck, cheek, penetrated an eyeball.

The body fell, and the Monster moved on.

They were here. He could smell them. Hiding.

He stomped through the old house, moving from room to room, following the scent of fear. He tracked them to a back bedroom. Huddled in a tiny closet. His prey was deep in the back, his woman boldly protecting him like a shield.

The Monster stared into her dark, defiant eyes. No fear. She had some beast in her too.

They moved at the same time. Her gun coughed as

he slapped it from her hand, snapping her wrist. She screamed, and the Monster bit her.

With his eyes trained deep in the darkness of the closet, he lifted her with one hand and hurled her behind him, across the room. Bone on wall rang out, but he never looked back. Instead he reached into the pit of the closet and grinned as his rock-breaking hand closed around hard flesh.

"Yo," Acqui cried. "It wasn't me, man! I swear to God. It was that niggah Rayz and 'em. I wasn't even there when it went down. Don't do this shit, man. I wasn't even there!"

Setting his gat on the ground, the Monster swung. Acqui screeched. Teeth flew, bones shattered, blood spurted. Fury raged and the Monster swung again. And again. And again, and again, and again. Crushing a nose-bone, tearing flesh from a skull, bringing darkness down on his prey.

"Not yet . . ." he muttered as the battered lump on the floor moaned and shuddered, close to death. Taking a knee, the Monster reached into his back pocket. A wrist-flick later a curved blade glinted in his hand.

"You like makin' smileys, huh?"

In a flash the knife sank into his prey's bloodied flesh,

laying his cheek open to the bone. The Monster paused momentarily to study his work. Dissatisfied, he went back for more.

"Not deep enough," he determined, then retraced his first slash. This time he carved a deep line in front of the ear and swung under the chin, then aimed the tip of his blade and pressed it deeply into Acqui's naked throat-meat.

The Monster didn't stop until his knife scraped neck-bone.

CHAPTER 10

War was being waged and Tony Santos's coordinated attack was hard and swift. Borne Reynolds was thought to be huddled in an apartment somewhere, naked and vulnerable. Two days earlier his Blake Avenue headquarters had been raided by the narcs sent by Malik, and a dozen of his top capos had gotten knocked and locked. That oily ass Borne had cut out and slipped through the net, but with key bricks missing from his wall of protection, his street game and his defense were pretty weak.

Death was in the air and residents huddled behind locked doors with their shades drawn. For such a crime-ridden area, there wasn't a police car in sight. Malik had called in a favor, and the detective he'd helped out of a jam with a white drug suspect one night had instructed his night patrol to go on an extended break until further notice.

They'd split up into fifteen- to twenty-man elements. Kadir headed one, Raheem another, and the three others followed the lead of Tony Santos's most trusted capos.

"Your shit straight?" Farad asked Tony, checking his load. Him and Finesse were accustomed to being generals, but tonight they were playing the soldier role. Instead of leading their own crews on a mission to annihilate Borne's low-level pawns, they'd chosen to ride out with the main element and go straight for the jugular. This was one night he didn't mind taking orders. Tony's loss had caused their loss, and their vengeance would be shared.

"Yeah," Tony answered. His men were armed to the max and positioned strategically along the border between Brownsville and East New York. Their orders were simple. Find Borne Reynolds and take him down. And wipe his crew out too.

For the next two hours back-alley war raged in East New York. Tony and his crew, accompanied by Farad, Finesse, and twenty of their most trusted Gs, split into factions and moved through the streets. Tenements, storefronts, and project apartments were invaded and cleared. They slumped every Borne soldier they rolled up on, having mercy on no one. The area surrounding the transit bridge between Brownsville and East

New York became an urban war zone with bullets spitting through the air and blood spilling out onto the streets.

Pushing farther east, they cornered Borne hiding in the back room of an Arab-owned candy store off Pennsylvania Avenue. The terrified owners lived above the store and had been dragged downstairs out of their apartment when Borne's crew commandeered the joint, seeking refuge from the overwhelming gunfire raging outside. The husband and wife were in their nightclothes, trembling behind the counter and checked by three of Borne's goonies holding big gats.

Farad fired through a window, and the cat he hit went down hard. The Arab couple screamed and ducked down behind the counter, seeking cover. Flanked by Finesse, Tony, and members of his crew, Farad charged inside, spraying lead across the entire room. Tony's boys pumped crazy shots, the noise deafening in its volume. But shit changed in a split second and Farad cursed out loud. One moment they were in control, aggressing their common enemy, and the next moment they were under attack, Borne's men rising up and swarming from a doorway concealed on the other side of the counter.

Behind him, Tony's boys opened their shit up on spray. Bullets whizzed past Farad's ears and he lunged for cover, the acrid gunpowder searing his nose.

He was caught in the cross fire. Targeted by stray bullets with no name on them. He rolled down an aisle and slid on his stomach, firing his piece with his arms extended in front of him. He was reaching into his holster for his second gat when a blinding heat seared across his back, and his gun fell from his hands.

"Finesse!" he tried to scream, but only a whisper escaped him. Farad rose up on his elbows and tried to drag himself across the floor, but another round tagged him in the shoulder and he went down flat on his face. For a moment the pain was almost unbearable. He bit his lip and tried to fight the waves of agony that threatened to swallow him, and for the most part it worked because seconds later darkness fell upon him and suddenly he felt no pain at all.

—   —   —   —

Borne got served.

Tony's crew regrouped and pushed forward. Clearing the front room and leaving piles of bodies behind

142

them. They found Borne down in the storage cellar. Him and two of his boys had rushed up a short flight of concrete stairs and were pushing desperately against the iron delivery flap-door that would allow them to emerge outside and onto the sidewalk.

It was gonna be a slaughter.

They were so outnumbered. Borne's goonie turned around and fired in fear, and one of Tony's right-hand Gs took a fall. The others began shooting in retaliation, but Tony silenced their weapons with a raised hand.

He walked right up on the three gangstas and popped two of them.

The last man standing trembled under Tony's killer glare.

Borne was filled with fear. He would have preferred the gun. Could have withstood that with honor. But the knife was a whole nother thing. Especially clenched in Tony's hand.

Tony moved in close, then mugged him, gripping his whole face. He mushed him down on the steps, then straddled him and pressed one knee into his throat. Tony stared into the eyes of his sister's killer, and rage washed over him in pulsating waves.

He had no words. Nothing in his vocabulary to

describe the depth of his fury. So he did what he did best. His self-expression was an art form in itself. It required skill, heart, and a total lack of compassion for his victim.

Tony held Borne by the throat and gazed at the rock he was about to sculpt. He'd create a masterpiece. A canvas. He examined angles and curves, the rough skin and uneven terrain. He held his knife like a paintbrush and prepared to make his first stroke.

And trapped in the bowels of the beast, Borne screamed.

━━ ━━ ━━ ━━

The sight of his brother lying in a pool of blood sent Finesse running. The floor was littered with bodies. Some were moving and moaning, others were still.

"Farad!" he shouted, slipping in blood as he ran down the aisle. He had stormed down into the cellar room without realizing his twin was down. It was only when Tony went to work on Borne and the torturous screaming began that he'd looked around for his brother.

Finesse wasn't letting Tony take it all. That muthafuckah knew to save some of that niggah for him and

Farad too. But when he looked for Farad so they could get a piece of Borne's ass before Tony completely disfigured him, a sinking feeling had slammed into him as he realized his brother was nowhere in sight.

He'd bounded back upstairs, ignoring the Puerto Rican cat who was watching the door, his eyes scanning the store for Farad.

He found him lying facedown. The back of his shirt was soaked through with blood, and he wasn't moving.

"Farad!"

Finesse turned his brother over and stared down into his still face. A moan of pain, fear, and rage ripped through him, as he slid his arms beneath his brother's body and sat him up, then lifted him. He staggered from the store. Feet sliding in blood, banging into display shelves and pumped with adrenaline.

"I got you, man," he muttered as Farad's head lolled on his neck, the full weight of his twin in his arms. Finesse stepped over bodies and crunched shards of glass under his feet, then stood on the sidewalk looking toward Brownsville.

Brookdale, was all he could think of. *I gotta get him to Brookdale.* If there was a hospital that was closer, he couldn't think of it. There wasn't a soul in sight. The people who lived nearby were smart enough to stay down when gunfire erupted, and Malik's man had all the cops out getting doughnuts. Farad moaned, and Finesse boosted him up. The warmth of his brother's blood dampened his clothes, and Finesse looked toward the avenue and braced himself for the long journey ahead.

EPILOGUE

Antwan paced the floors of Brookdale Hospital, wondering what was taking so long. He glanced at his watch every few minutes, then again at the closed doors at the end of the hall.

At seven minutes past two the hydraulic doors whooshed and swung outward. A young black nurse appeared, pretty dreadlocks flowing around her heart-shaped face.

"Hey," Antwan said, grinning widely.

"What's poppin'?" asked the younger man being pushed toward him in the wheelchair.

The men shook hands briefly, then Antwan reached down and put his arms around Farad and held him close.

They'd almost lost him. The bullets he took had ripped through his spine, nearly demolishing his intestines on their deadly path through his body.

Antwan had barely understood what Finesse was telling him when he called from the emergency room.

When he realized Farad had been shot, shame immediately overtook him. Instead of watching out for his brothers, he'd become a monster. Invincible. Impenetrable. He'd been so consumed with exacting wrath that he had allowed rage to rule him and put the lives of his brothers in the path of vengeance.

Farad had endured hours of surgery, and each of his brothers were at his bedside when he opened his eyes.

"Bad?" he'd asked in a hoarse whisper.

Antwan had nodded as Finesse touched his twin's arm and Malik moved closer to his side.

"You're paralyzed," Antwan told him simply, giving it to him all at once without any pretenses. "From the waist down. Could be permanent, might not be. The doctors said it's day to day. We gotta wait and see."

Farad had closed his eyes momentarily, and when he opened them again Antwan saw real strength there.

"Borne?"

Kadir made a noise in his throat and Finesse shook his head and answered the question. "Murked. Slumped. Cheese, my niggah. Shredded cheese."

"Yeah," Raheem added, "that kid Rayz gonna get his too. He's getting sent to Elmira. Tony got a crew of

Puerto Ricans runnin' shit up there and they already planning his welcoming party."

Farad nodded, satisfied.

And now, two months after his shooting, the pretty black nurse smiled as Antwan moved behind his brother's wheelchair and grasped the handholds. Farad had endured several weeks of physical therapy, and today would be the first time he felt the warmth of the sun since being wheeled into the hospital flat on his back.

"Where's the posse?" Farad asked as they rode downstairs in the elevator.

"They're all here," Antwan told him.

Farad nodded, then spoke again. "Where's the Monster?"

It took Antwan a long time to answer, but when he did his voice came out strong and sure. "He's gone, man. He died the night they brought you in here."

Thirty minutes later Antwan and his five brothers were riding through the gates of Evergreen Cemetery. Finesse was behind the wheel of the custom van they'd purchased, and when they arrived in the Gibron section he pulled over and helped Raheem unfold the wheelchair and settle Farad down into it.

They walked together over to the plot that had

been in their family for the past eighteen years. Standing at the grave site in silence, they stared down at the headstone that read simply, "Father" "Mother" "Baby Brother."

"Pops was a crazy cat," Antwan reminisced, the fall sun warming his face.

Farad chuckled in his chair. "Yeah, he was. He was a wild dude who did his thing regardless . . . but he dug his little cats, though. We was his lucky seven, remember? He used to say he could bet his last dime on his seven boys."

"I miss Mama," Malik blurted out. "If she was here she would be mad as hell with all of us."

Antwan agreed. Each of them had stood around her bed on that last night. They'd put their bonded word on her soul and sent her out of this world with some bone-deep promises that they had all failed to live by.

Finesse looked down at his twin and put Antwan's thoughts into words.

"We failed her, man. We swore we would keep her with us. Swore we wouldn't let the streets suck the life outta us."

He put his hand on his twin's shoulder.

"We still some hard niggahs, bruh. Soldiers. But we outta this shit, man. Cool?"

And when Farad nodded, Finesse turned to Antwan. "Your offer still good, man? You still thinkin' on expanding them barbershops and breaking off a few franchises?"

Antwan grinned. They said God worked in mysterious ways, and this change of heart was one mystery he was gonna roll with and not question.

"Yeah, I might wanna get down on summa that too," Kadir spoke up. "It's getting hot in A.C., man. I gotta find another hustle. Mama would turn over in her grave if the same thing that happened to Daddy ended up happening to me."

Still battling his guilt, Raheem gave his younger brother some love, then gazed toward the grave and spoke for the first time since they'd arrived. "We didn't watch out for Baby Brother like you wanted us to, Mama. But we loved him. You know we did. And even though he's gone, the rest of us are still here swinging, and that means we can still make something outta what we got left."

Antwan gathered his brothers in his arms and agreed.

TURN THE PAGE FOR EXCERPTS OF MORE G-UNIT BOOKS

from 50 Cent

THE SKI MASK WAY

By 50 Cent
and K. Elliott

The fruit-punch-red Impala had gold Dayton rims. The car gleamed so much, you could see your reflection in the hood. The interior was cream-colored leather. The car had been totally restored. The Impala was the only one that Butter owned and he cherished it. He and Seven sat on the hood of his car, smoking purple haze, listening to Mobb Deep's "Shook Ones Part I."

"This was my shit back in the day and those niggas was from round my way," Seven said.

Butter puffed the blunt. "You knew them?"

Seven reached for the blunt. "Well, not exactly. My manz in'nem used to hang with Prodigy; but, naw, I ain't know them, but I seen them a few times."

"I listen to them, when I'm about to do a lick, you know?" Butter pulled out a .380 and cocked the hammer. "It gets my adrenaline going, you know?"

"Man, put that gun away," Seven said.

"What, nigga? You scared of guns? How the fuck is you from New York and you afraid of guns?"

"Naw; I ain't afraid of guns—just high, careless niggas with guns."

Butter put the gun on safety.

"I didn't know niggas in the South was into that Mobb Deep shit."

Butter looked confused. He didn't say anything, he just puffed. Finally he couldn't control his thoughts or his tongue.

"You know what? Y'all New York niggas always think that we slow down here. I can relate to Mobb Deep."

"I feel ya," Seven said. "Calm down, son. I mean, I ain't mean it like that." Seven did think southern niggas were slow, once upon a time, before he'd gone to Virginia. He'd met some real gangsters in Virginia. Butter seemed to be through. He'd met him at a temp agency where they both were applying for a job and started talking. After a fifeen-minute conversation he realized they had a lot in common: They both were street niggas and ex-cons.

"So what your all-time favorite gangster movie?"

"Dead Presidents."

"I expected you to say *King of New York, New Jack City, Menace II Society*. Never did I expect you to say this."

Butter inhaled the haze and then coughed. "Yeah, I liked that movie."

"I liked *Paid in Full,* myself," Seven said.

Butter coughed again. "Yeah, that shit was crazy; those mufukas was making a lot of money."

"You know what my favorite scene was?"

"What?"

"You know the scene where Mitch calls Rico and tells him he has coke and Rico flips and kills his man for the work?"

"Why is that your favorite scene?" Butter asked.

"Because the lesson learned is niggas will kill you for life-changing money. My daddy always told me two things: Your friends will kill you for the right price, and every bad guy likes to think of himself as good," Seven said.

"Was you and your pops smoking weed when he told you that shit? Sounds like that weed philosophy," Butter commented.

"That's real talk, man, from a man who's doing life in the pen."

"That's why you gotta watch everybody." Butter blew out a huge smoke ring, pulled the gun out, cocked it again, then kissed the barrel. "I'm 'bout hit a lick tonight, man. I needs some money in a major way."

"I ain't got shit myself, and that motherfuckin' baby mama is nagging the shit out of me. My son is two and can't walk—he needs physical therapy. The bitch ain't got no insurance." Seven thought about his boy and other problems he was having. He hardly ever had money. Sometimes he would detail cars for hustlers but he didn't have any real paper—not like he was used to—hell, before he'd gotten locked up he had thousands of dollars on him at all times. Now it was down to this petty-assed car washing—he felt like a sucker.

Butter sat back on the Impala. Young Jeezy was now

coming from the Chevy. "You know what? I thought you were locked up three years ago in Virginia. Right."

"Yeah."

"How the fuck did you get her pregnant, anyway? I mean, I was thinking about that shit one night. I was high as fuck, sitting outside, looking up at the sky and shit. You know that's when you high; you have the strangest thoughts."

"Now that's got to be a weed-induced thought."

"I was on that purple haze and my mind was just racing and shit, and I was thinking of all kinds of stupid shit."

"Well, Adrian was actually a guard that I met while I was on the inside. I started banging her and the warden got wind of it. Fired her and put me in solitary confinement," Seven said.

Butter's eyes grew wide. "Nigga, quit lying."

"I'm serious. One thing about me, man, is that I've never had a problem with the ladies, I've always been able to pull them." Seven was indeed a ladies' man. Very attractive dark smooth skin, wavy hair; his body was well-defined and his teeth were eggshell white. The women loved him.

"Damn, that's an amazing story," Butter said.

"Yeah, man. That's how the shit went down. I got her pregnant. We kept in touch while I was in prison and she moved to Charlotte, N.C., so that's why I relocated here."

"Why did you relocate here?"

Seven inhaled the blunt. "Damn, nigga, you a news reporter? Motherfucker, why so many questions—you the FBI or something?"

"Naw, just making sure you ain't FBI," Butter replied.

"I mean I got three sisters and three brothers in New York, but I ain't really fucking with them like that. I mean, the whole time I was down only one of my sisters came to visit me so I ain't really have no reason to go back to New York and I ain't going back to Virginia cuz all my niggas locked up."

"Damn. You came all the way down here not knowing anybody."

"I wasn't afraid. The only thing I was worried about was that bitch tripping, and she tripped and put me out. But it's okay, I got my own room in the boardinghouse and I got some pussy, so I'm good."

"Nigga, you must not be used to having money."

"Now that's where you're wrong at. I made a lot of money. Ran with a fucking crew—and most of them niggas that I ran with are either dead or in jail."

Butter rolled another blunt, lit it and inhaled, then blew another smoke ring before coughing loudly.

"What the fuck were y'all doing?"

"Coke, heroin, e-pills . . . all types shit."

"I can't believe that shit, man, cuz it just seems like you are so content with being an average motherfucker."

"Nigga, you average," Seven said.

"But I ain't never got no real money, nigga. I bet y'all seen millions."

Seven thought back. A few years ago he was driving Porsches, BMWs and shit with expensive rims. Ever since he'd been released from prison a year ago, it had only been a bus pass. He really wanted money too, but he didn't know anybody who would give him drugs. He was in Charlotte. Nobody knew him. This was both good and bad. It was good because he didn't have a reputation to keep, but it was bad because he couldn't get anybody in Charlotte to supply him.

Butter passed Seven the gun. "Got this motherfucker for two rocks, nigga, it was brand-new in the box."

"What you mean you got it for two rocks, you ain't no hustler."

"I know but I have drugs because I'm the type of motherfucker that takes shit from the dope boyz, you know, if they making money I'm making money because they have to give me money or else I'll rob they punk ass. I actually took the dope from a nigga, gave it to another motherfucker for the gun and when I got the gun I robbed the nigga that sold me the gun and got my rocks back . . . that's how ya boy Butter gets down."

Seven laughed but he really didn't think that was funny. He'd been around niggas like Butter before and knew he could only trust him as far as he could see him.

"So—do you want to help me with this lick?"

"So, who is this cat, Caesar? And does he have money?"

"He has a Colombian plug, and word in the street is he gets those bricks for thirteen five. He just bought this stripper bitch a Benz for her birthday."

"How can we get at him?" Seven wanted to know. He remembered the days when he was dealing in Richmond, Virginia. He knew that the streets talk, especially in the South; news spread like wildfire. Things that were just ordinary conversation could be made into major news. He also knew that whoever Caesar was, it wasn't going to be easy to get to him.

"One thing you have to always remember is that most of these major drug dealers are cowards. You don't have to worry about them. It's the niggas around them that you have to worry about; the enforcer-type niggas. Those are the hungry mufuckas that will do something to you," Butter pointed out.

"Exactly. I know this. I mean I ain't never stuck nobody up, but I know the fuckin' streets. I know legendary stickup kids in New York. I'm talking about kidnap-your-mom type niggas, son."

Butter chuckled to himself. He never understood why New Yorkers called everybody "son." A motherfucker could be seventy years old and still be called son.

"I know what ya mean. But—back to the business. You with me or not?"

Seven thought for a moment and took a puff of the

blunt. He knew that if what Butter said was true, he would be doing a lot better than he had been doing. Hell. He lived in a boardinghouse with twelve other sweaty men and one crackhead woman. He wanted out of that place more than he did prison. He envisioned taking kilos of coke from the drug dealer with the Colombian connection. "Yeah. I'm down, son."

Butter tossed him a pair of gloves and a ski mask and a sawed-off pump shotgun. "Let's get that money the fast way the ski mask way."

"The ski mask way . . . Hell yeah," Seven said. He and Butter high-fived.

The subdivision was called Peaceful Oaks. A quiet neighborhood in the southeastern part of Charlotte. It was predominantely white, which meant they had to be very cautious. White people called the police at the slightest bit of suspicion. Two black men rolling through suburbia after midnight was not a good look. Butter and Seven rolled through the neighborhood looking out for Good Samaritans—people that wanted to be on the news saying that they tipped the police.

Caesar's street was Peaceful Way Drive. Butter went one street over, to Peaceful Pine Drive, and parked the car in the driveway of an abandoned house.

He and Seven hopped over the privacy fence in the backyard into Caesar's backyard and looked around, but didn't see anybody. Then Seven saw the sign that read ADT in front of the door.

"He has an alarm. Man. What do we do about that?"

"He has a baby, too."

Seven looked confused. "What the fuck does that have to do with anything?"

"Don't worry about this shit. I've done it before. I got this player."

Seven put on the mask and the gloves. He thought about prison; the sick old men there, the perverts, the liars and the snitches. He didn't want to go back to that place. They went around front. Nobody noticed them and the street was dark.

"On the count of three, I'm going to kick in the door. I want you to go in one room and I go in the other, just in case there is somebody else in the house."

"Nigga, you've done this shit before for real?" Seven said.

Butter's face hardened. "This ain't no fuckin' game to me, man. I need to eat."

"Okay. Let's do it."

Butter kicked the door in and ran into the first bedroom.

Seven ran into the second bedroom and found a man and a woman on the floor, naked. He pointed the gun at the man. "Okay, I need you to get the fuck up and your bitch to stay on the floor with her hands on her head."

The man was shaking and it looked as if tears were in his eyes. *Damn, what a bitch-assed nigga,* Seven thought.

"Nobody is going to get hurt as long as you do what the fuck I say."

Butter walked into the room with a little boy wearing Elmo pajamas.

"Look what I have."

The little boy began to cry.

The alarm went off. Caesar said, "The police will be here soon. You don't want to go to jail, do you?"

Seven said sarcastically, "Yeah. That what we came here for . . . to get caught and go to jail." He slapped Caesar with the barrel of the gun.

"Don't you say a motherfuckin' thing."

He walked Caesar into the hallway to the alarm keypad.

"Disarm the alarm," Seven ordered.

Caesar punched in the code.

The telephone rang. Butter picked it up without answering it. The caller ID said ADP.

"The fuckin' alarm company."

"Well, we knew they had an alarm," Seven said.

"Don't worry," Butter said, and he walked the phone over to Caesar with the infant still in his hand, crying. "Tell them everything is okay," Butter said. "If you try some slick shit, I'll blow your fucking block off, nigga."

"Hello," Caesar said.

A female voice said, "This is ADP. Is everything okay?"

"Yes, everything is fine. I just didn't get to the alarm pad on time."

"Okay. What is your password?"

"My password?"

Butter clenched his teeth.

"Tell the bitch your password or else it's going to be a fuckin' bloodbath in this motherfucker. I promise you, man."

"The password is *rubber*."

The little boy started crying louder.

"Okay, sir. Are you sure everything is okay?"

"Yes; everything is fine, ma'am."

"Do I hear a child crying?"

"That's my son. The alarm scared him."

"Okay, sir. You have a good night."

Butter snatched the phone out of Caesar's hand and terminated the call.

"Okay, man. Where the fuck is the dope, nigga?"

"Ain't no dope here, man."

"Okay, motherfucker. You think I'm stupid?" Seven said through clenched teeth. "You think I believe you worked for this house and that fat-assed Benz you got outside? You think that I think this fine-assed bitch is with you for you good looks?" Seven looked at the female, who was still facedown and shaking nervously.

"Where the fuck is the cash?" Butter said.

"I'm telling you I ain't got shit."

"Nigga, you ain't gonna have no fuckin' son if you don't give us what we want."

"Please don't hurt my baby," the woman said, then stood.

Seven pointed the gun at her.

"Bitch, get back on the floor."

"Where the fuck is the dope?" Butter repeated.

"There ain't no dope here."

Butter walked over to the window and pulled the curtains back. "I'ma count to three. If you don't give me some dope or some money, this little boy is going out of the window."

"Put the child down," Seven said as he thought about his own little boy. He never had a soft spot for kids until he had brought Tracey into the world.

He and Butter made eye contact before Butter said, "Nigga, you don' tell me what the fuck to do. I'm telling this motherfucker if I don't get what the fuck I want, this little boy is going out of the window."

The woman stood and Seven aimed the gun at her again. "Get your ass back on the floor."

"No. Please, please don't hurt my baby. I'll tell you where the money is."

Seven cocked the hammer of the gun. "Well, tell me where the godamned money is, then."

"Please, put my son down first."

Butter put the child on the bed.

The woman went into the closet and pulled out a large green gym bag. Butter unzipped the bag and saw bundles of money. He zipped the bag back up.

"Okay; where's the dope, bitch?"

"There really ain't no dope in here. I swear to God," the woman said.

"Okay."

Butter stepped out of the closet.

"Bring him to me," Butter said to Seven.

Seven walked Caesar over.

"Okay, nigga. Where ya fucking car keys at, and ya guns and shit?"

The woman got the keys from the nightstand and handed them to Butter.

Butter duct-taped Caesar's hands and feet together and handcuffed the woman to the bed.

The baby was still crying. Seven walked over to him, ran his fingers through the toddler's hair and said, "It's going to be okay."

They left with the money.

DEATH BEFORE DISHONOR

By 50 Cent
and Nikki Turner

As Trill cruised through the little hick town of Ashland, he consciously abided by all the laws. It didn't matter, though, because the sheriff was sure he had hit the lotto when he spotted his mark: a young black male driving a $60,000 truck. The Hummer happened to be Sheriff Bowman Body's dream truck. A truck he could only dream of having with his salary, and he despised the fact that some punk who probably never even finished high school was riding around in it.

Trill could have been wearing a priest's collar, but as far as Bowman Body was concerned, he was a drug dealer and a prime victim of the monthly driving citation quota. Before Trill could think twice, the sheriff's blue lights were bouncing off of his rearview mirror.

"Fuck!" Trill shouted. He beat his hand on the steering wheel as he spat the word out. He quickly looked down and, after making sure that his secret hiding place was secure, then pulled over. He watched from his side mirror as the small, thin-featured sheriff approached the car. His walk was like Forrest Gump but his look was the Terminator, coming to devour.

"License and registration, boy!" the sheriff said with

authority as he knocked on the driver's side window.

Trill rolled down the window halfway. "No problem, Officer," he responded, and leaned forward to the glove box to retrieve his registration.

"Freeze!" The sheriff drew his gun and stuck his hand inside the car.

Stunned, Trill slowly eased back into the driver's seat until he felt the tip of the sheriff's revolver at his temple.

"I was going for my registration, man," Trill said slowly. "Don't most people keep their registration in the glove box?"

"You trying to get fresh with me, nigger?" The sheriff cocked his gun.

Trill could feel his blood boiling. Given the opportunity, he would leave the racist redneck stinkin' on the hood of his own police cruiser for his fellow officers to scrape him off.

"You would think that you niggers would know the drill by now, and have these things prepared," the sheriff drawled boldly. "As much shit as y'all stay in, you'd think y'all would pin the damn registration to your collars. Now slowly," Bowman Body said, "open the glove box and retrieve the registration." He paused before adding, "And I said slowly, not like you grabbing for the last piece of chicken out of a bucket of Colonel Sanders."

Trill smelled the scent of trouble like shit from a three-hundred-pound man who just got an enema. He knew Barney Fife was gon' fuck with him until he came up with a reason good enough to stick him. Trill was fully aware that the four thousand grams of crack cocaine in his hiding spot was 3,400 grams more than enough to get him a mandatory life sentence in a federal penitentiary. His instincts told him that he didn't want to trust his life on the chance that this hillbilly didn't impound the truck and stumble upon the stash box. He had to make a move. His next move would be crucial. A convicted felon caught with four kilos of crack cocaine was not a good look. He couldn't take that chance; that was reason enough to give Bowman Body a run for his money. And he intended to do just that.

Trill grabbed the registration from the glove box and turned to hand it to the sheriff. When the sheriff reached inside the truck with his free hand and grabbed hold of the registration, Trill quickly hit the switch to roll the window up while he floored the accelerator at the same time. The powerful Hummer snatched the sheriff off his feet so fast he dropped the pistol, screaming while Trill put the pedal to the metal.

"Who the fuck reaching now? Get yo' hand out the chicken box, cracker!" Trill screamed at Bowman Body. "Get yo' shit out my chicken box, motherfucker!" His adrenaline was pumping, having the upper hand. He knew if he was caught he was gone for life. So he was going out like a real-live gangsta—with a mean fight.

He drove the Humdinger like he was on safari in Africa; the sheriff hung from the side of the car, holding on for dear life, slamming into the door every now and then as the truck dragged him at sixty miles an hour down the road. He went from Barney Fife to Barney Rubble as he ran alongside the automobile.

Bowman Body was swinging from side to side, praying and calling out every scripture in the Bible he'd ever known from his childhood days of going to Vacation Bible School. Once Trill felt like he was deep enough in the sticks and had room and leeway to run and hide, he pushed the window's button down to release the sheriff and slammed on the brakes, throwing the sheriff face-first to the ground.

Trill knew that the truck was going to be hot and keeping the beautiful machine would not be an option. This was most likely the only deserted stretch of road he was going to find. He grabbed a piece just in case he had to go to war, pulled off the road and got out of the truck. When Trill opened up the door, Bowman Body was crawling on his belly like a frontline soldier. He was relentless and wasn't going to give up easily. He managed to lunge forward and grab Trill's leg to try to slow him down. Trill laughed at first. He couldn't believe the motherfucker was on his heels. But after he tried to wiggle his leg loose to no avail, he got pissed off.

Trill kicked the sheriff in his face with his new Timbs. Bowman Body's head hit a rock, causing him to bleed like Rick Flair in a cage match. Blood gushed out all over the pavement. Trill didn't waste time. Although his shoes had blood on them, he took off running like a jaguar in the wild. He was mad that he didn't have on the fresh Jordans that he copped earlier from the mall, but Timbs were good in any kind of weather.

It was unlikely that the police would find the drugs, but if they did, it wouldn't matter. Trill's only concern at this point was to get away. He took comfort in knowing that the registered owner of the vehicle didn't know him from a can of paint. He'd paid a friend to pay a friend $10,000 to put the Hummer in their name. Maybe the best $10,000 he'd ever spent; it pays to think ahead.

It felt like hours as Trill trudged through the trees, mud, rocks and small streams of water. Out of breath and panting, he found a tree to rest against. He knew that he would be there until sundown. Some hunter stopped to help the sheriff, and of course by now backup was on the way, but at least Trill had gotten a fairly decent head start. But no sooner had Trill thought the fading sun was his answer than he heard a sound that put him on the run again. And he needed to move fast. Trill knew he had to shed some weight. As much as he hated to part with it, the first thing to go was his brand-new chinchilla jacket.

The sound of bloodhounds let Trill know that backup and probably some deputized citizens with shotguns were on the scent of his trail. He wasn't too much worried about the bloodhounds; his main concern was them redneck hillbillies who could smell a nigga a mile away. The manhunt was on.

As the pursuit continued, Trill knew that they

were closing in on him. Not only was the sound of the hounds getting closer, he could hear the hum of a helicopter entering the area. He couldn't see it yet, but the sound of the whirling blades were distinctive. And just because he couldn't see it didn't mean that it couldn't see him. He knew he was doomed. But he trudged through the woods anyway, hoping no one in the distant houses would see him and give him up. He had no idea where he was going or where he'd end up. The only destination he had in mind was to get the fuck out of redneck county!

———   ———   ———   ———

As Sunni stood in her kitchen warming up some leftover hot wings from the day before, she went to wash off the sauce that had gotten on her hands. As she looked out of the window over the sink, she could have sworn that she saw something. It was dark, and the light was on in the kitchen, so she could barely see. She flipped the light switch off, allowing her a better view of the rear of her house, and there it was again. It was a person; a black man, and then she zeroed in on the helicopter overhead. When she looked back down from the helicopter, she found herself staring into the eyes of someone in her backyard. She jumped, and a scream slipped out, but then she felt a sense of familiarity. It was the same guy from the Hummer earlier, the one who had given her a visual orgasm at the stoplight.

She knew for a fact that he wasn't volunteering on the manhunt—a black man in this neck of the woods, after sundown? Hell no! Oh, she thought, this brother is definitely being hunted. Sunni knew that if he was caught only one of two things could happen: one, he would be shot dead on the spot, another black man out of the running; or two, he would go straight to jail and the key would be thrown away.

Guydamn, Sunni contemplated. *Why'd he have to end up on my doorstep? What am I supposed to do?*

As she watched him looking for a way out, somewhere to run, his face clammy with sweat, her heart went out to him. She quickly ran to the back door, unlocked it and called out, "Come on, come on, I got you!" She waved her arm, motioning him to hurry up.

She shook her head, knowing that she had let her emotions override her intellect for a man once again. Hopefully, this time it won't turn out as bad for her as it did the last time.

Upon seeing the door open, Trill ran inside. He couldn't believe it. He knew that it was only a matter of seconds before they had his black butt hemmed in. This lady being here at the right place, at the right time—he didn't know if it was a setup or what. But for now he was grateful to be able to get some heat and a spot to hide. She slammed the door shut, locking both the security door and the entry door.

He inhaled deeply, trying to catch his breath. "Damn, you saved my ass. Anybody see me?"

Sunni looked out the still open blinds in the kitchen. She separated the blinds just enough to peek out. The coast appeared to be clear. Sunni then closed all the blinds in her house and drew the drapes.

"You can hang out here if you need to," Sunni said flatly when she returned to the kitchen. "You need to use the phone or something?"

"Naw, I just need to lay low and chill for a minute," Trill said and then plopped down on her oversized yellow chaise, exhausted, dehydrated and hungry. Then he thought again. "You got a cell?"

Sunni nodded as she reached for her cell and handed it to him. She listened as he gave someone demands to report his truck stolen. After Trill ended the call, he sat there with a bit of slight anxiety, thinking about the stash box, wondering if the tow company would find it and rip it off. Sunni noticed that his mind was somewhere else, so she tried to redirect his attention.

"Well, I was just about to eat some hot wings," she said casually. "Have some?"

"You got something cold to drink?" he asked. Writing off any negative thoughts about the drugs being gone, he knew he had the best secret hiding place money could buy.

"Sure." She walked over to a cabinet that sat behind the yellow love seat. She opened the refrigerator, introducing a complete stock of liquor, most of which hadn't been uncapped. She then hollered back to Trill.

"I have Coke, Sprite, Corona, Hennessey, Moët,

Remy, Grey Goose, orange juice, basically whatever you want," Sunni said, naming the drinks as she scanned the fridge then glanced over to her bar.

"Hennie's good, give me a shot of that on ice." He could feel her eyes burning into him, so he added, "Please."

As she grabbed a glass from the cabinet and poured Trill's drink, she decided that maybe she'd have a drink, too. No use in having dude drinking alone, she thought. After pouring herself a Grey Goose and cranberry, she headed to the kitchen and grabbed some ice from the freezer. When she closed the freezer door and went to turn around, Trill was already standing in the kitchen. He pulled off his sweater and tossed it across the chair beside him as if he lived there. Trill's body caught Sunni off guard. Seeing him in that black wife beater, she could see he'd definitely spent a lot of time working on his body. *Penitentiary body,* she thought as he drank the Henni like it was a shot.

"You mind?" he asked, referring to the wing he had grabbed off the plate on the table. Then with the same cockiness, he dipped it in the homemade sauce she'd made earlier.

"No, go on," she replied as she watched him take a bite of the wing.

The way he sucked that chicken sent chills up her spine. She watched him put the wing in his mouth and pull off all the meat—with one bite, it was down to the bone.

Look for the newest urban erotic tale
from bestselling author

NOIRE

THONG ON FIRE

From the streets to the sheets,
Thong on Fire spins the torn-from-the-headlines
story of Saucy Sarita Robinson—a sassy video
vixen whose grimy street capers lift her up to
the top of her game, then slam
her down. **Hard**.

Coming in March wherever books are sold or at
www.simonsays.com.

ATRIA BOOKS
A Division of Simon & Schuster
A CBS COMPANY

50 CENT conquered the streets, the music charts, and the bestseller lists with his memoir *FROM PIECES TO WEIGHT.* But he's just getting started.

50 Cent
Announces

G Unit Books

Printed in the United States
By Bookmasters